Allegiance

ALSO BY GURNEY NORMAN

Divine Right's Trip

Kinfolks

Ancient Creek

Allegiance

Stories

by

GURNEY NORMAN

OLD COVE PRESS

LEXINGTON, KENTUCKY

Published by
Old Cove Press • oldcove.com

Distributed by
Ohio University Press • ohioswallow.com

Hardback ISBN 978-1-7352242-9-9
Electronic ISBN 978-1-7352242-8-2

Paperback edition ©2022 by Gurney Norman
Paperback ISBN 978-1-956855-02-9

First Edition

Earlier versions of some of the stories in *Allegiance* have been
published by Larkspur Press, and in literary journals, including
*Appalachian Heritage, Appalachian Journal, CoEvolution Quarterly,
Iron Mountain Review, Mountain Life & Work, Mountain Review,
Now & Then, Pine Mountain Sand & Gravel, and Southern Quarterly.*

Allegiance was designed by Nyoka Hawkins.
The type is Weiss Antiqua, designed by Emil Rudolf Weiss
in 1928, and Alisal, designed by Matthew Carter in 1995.
Cover painting by Pam Oldfield Meade, 2021.
Grateful acknowledgment to Stephanie Adams and Sharon Hatfield.

Library of Congress Cataloging-in-Publication Data
Names: Norman, Gurney, 1937– author.
Title: Allegiance : stories / Gurney Norman.
Description: First edition. | Lexington, Kentucky : Old Cove Press, [2021]
Identifiers: LCCN 2021016384 (print) | LCCN 2021016385 (ebook) |
ISBN 9781735224299 (hardcover) | ISBN 9781735224282 (pdf)
Subjects: LCGFT: Short stories. | Essays.
Classification: LCC PS3564.O57 A79 2021 (print) |
LCC PS3564.O57 (ebook) | DDC 818/.5409–dc23
LC record available at https://lccn.loc.gov/2021016384
LC ebook record available at https://lccn.loc.gov/2021016385

For Nyoka and Gwynne

Contents

Epilogue

—————◆—————

Foreword

"I SAT THERE BLIND a long time but gradually my eyes adjusted and several years went by." A lifetime goes by, in fact, and we are along for the trip in Gurney Norman's *Allegiance*. Wilgus Collier is the blinded five-year-old in "The Photograph," a masterful story near the beginning of *Allegiance*. Norman opens the book with a three-page prose poem, "Allegiance," a lyric overture to the southern Appalachian Mountains that names and blesses the roads and towns and creeks and railroad tracks, the cemeteries and hills of his homeplace.

But the soaring mood is short-lived. The formative memories rendered in stories like "The Photograph," "Karo," and "The Wreck" are forged of painful realities, narrated by a consciousness of intense awareness. *Allegiance* is the autobiography of that consciousness.

The opening stories surface randomly, as memories might present themselves. This disjuncture of time is purposeful: all time exists at once in a consciousness doomed (blessed?) with the ability—or necessity—of living an entire life's events simultaneously. In "Main Street," Wilgus, grown to adulthood, returns to eastern Kentucky and his hometown of Blaine:

> Walking up Main Street in the early morning, past
> Neely's and Pogue's, the Rexall Store, Johnson's Hard-
> ware, Tots 'n' Teens and Preston's Dry Goods...Wilgus
> sees himself in the very panes of glass he'd seen himself

in when he was three. He's fifty-three now, lumpy-looking in his winter coat...unfamiliar to himself in these
familiar windows, slightly shocked to see himself at all.

Norman unleashes a *tour de force* of writing styles and techniques
across the collection: lyric meditations, narrative realism, anecdotes,
dreamscapes, Jack Tales, and streams of consciousness. The book
as a whole works by accretion and juxtaposition. Its stories, the
product of years of writing, strike many different tones at different
depths, as stanzas might in a long poem. Brilliantly arranged, each
piece shapes our understanding of what has gone before and what
comes after, prisms enlarging the effect of the whole.

The gathering force of the writing bears fruit in three central
stories, "Welcome to New York," "The Dream," and "Quilt Thread."
Each treads the thin membrane between real and surreal. "Welcome
to New York," the pivotal piece, finds Wilgus broke and stranded,
"glad to be alone...disconnected from personal time or history."
For two days he rides the subway and the Staten Island Ferry, goes
to movies, drinks coffee, stretching twenty-four dollars and a stash
of uppers into a routine that comes to define him briefly. Shaken
loose of his home ground, stripped of the circumstance of his stories, and left with only the narratives that have held him all of his
life, Wilgus ends up telling his stories in a museum:

> I tried to explain it all to the lady in the museum...
> [who] seemed willing to listen although she said not a
> word to me. I told her about...the subway and the ferry
> and Fellini and the million fish....I told her about the
> bridge, about walking on it as the sun came up...about
> Whitman and Wolfe and Crane. Then stories of my
> family in Kentucky started spilling out...

Narrated among "the portraits and statues and suits of armor all around," Wilgus's stories and the people in them escape the events that constrained them. Expressive as an antiquarian vase or frieze, the stories stand, freed from the teller's need to explain or be understood.

If "Welcome to New York" is the pivot of the book, "The Dream" and "Quilt Thread" are its heart—free-associative mergings of place and family and self, outside time. Wilgus dreams a shining thread woven through the landscape and through his memories of his parents, whose lives he enters now from a place larger than personal history. In an act of compassionate imagination, the writing extends itself tenderly toward these two people who, crippled by their own wounds, wounded Wilgus, and honors their separate stories. It is an act of forgiveness that refuses to "prettify" what history (personal or cultural) has devastated, even as it enfolds what has been destroyed.

Appalachian poet, writer, and scholar Jim Wayne Miller was fond of intoning that "All literature is local somewhere." And, of course, writers like Chekhov, Kafka, Tolstoy, Welty, and Faulkner wrote a local literature. What distinguishes "regional writing" from literature of lasting worth is not a matter of place, but of vision. Gurney Norman is a visionary writer for whom the local provides a means to imagine and embody the whole.

Norman's genius is to write a small and "ordinary" story. The writing doesn't seem to be doing anything special, yet leaves the reader deeply affected. Norman is the kind of writer whose stories you put down, thinking, "Well, then," as if not much has happened. Until a day, a week, years later, you realize that an image, a mood, a situation from them has lodged itself in your psyche and lives there. *Kinfolks: The Wilgus Stories* and *Divine Right's Trip* did that to me:

FOREWORD

Fat Monroe's merciless teasing and Divine Right's Uncle Emmit's "rabbit shit" plan to restore ecological devastation in Appalachia render the kind of situation a lesser writer might not articulate. Each spoke something of this midwestern farm girl's fears and hopes. *Allegiance* completes the trilogy with its declaration of identity with and love for Appalachia, its assertion that Wilgus's (and Norman's) origin in and experience of these mountains embody the cosmos.

LEATHA KENDRICK

Allegiance

Allegiance

I PLEDGE ALLEGIANCE to Rockhouse Creek in Letcher County, however far I roam. I pledge to always visit my family's graves, brother, mother, father, grandparents, aunts, uncles, cousins, scattered in the hills. I will always drive the old roads I traveled in my youth and still travel every chance I get, especially Route 7 from Jeff to Sandy Hook, through old coal camps and towns like Wayland where our football team in 1952 played a pretty good game even though we lost. I pledge allegiance to Highway 119 across Letcher County and into Harlan town to meet Highway 421, which goes south across Black Mountain to Lee County, Virginia, and Route 58 through Powell Valley to Cumberland Gap. I pledge allegiance to Cudjo's Cave in the saddle of the Gap, to the huge stalactite deep inside the cave that's been hanging from a high vaulted ceiling for eighty million years. And to the memories of former times and local places—world of two-lane roads and single-lane bridges, certain curves and intersections and mere spots by the road where significant things happened, the curve where my brother died, the spot by the small bridge over Cane Creek where I stood with my father as we waited for the bus that would take him back to the VA hospital, the last time I saw him alive, I pledge allegiance. And to the little roadside stores where you could buy a baloney sandwich and a dope for twenty cents, the people in the stores talking easily,

3

laughing, catching up on each other's news; then walking along the railroad tracks, carrying their groceries home, the smell of coal smoke in the air, children scrambling around the hillsides, finding old house foundations, stone chimneys standing lonely in a field, rusted bedsprings in the weeds, old mining works, old slate dumps, forgotten hillside cemeteries overgrown by kudzu vines, the daily life of the coal camps, men walking up the holler, going to work, carrying their dinner buckets under their arms, graceful in their walking; all day the loaded coal gons rolling away from the tipple, forty gons in a train, thick black smoke, steam clouds and ashes blowing back from the engine, coal-fired boilers turning the water to steam, and down the line, passing kids playing on the riverbank who wave at the engineers, then in the rain walk across the trestle above the swollen river, water pouring out of the ground of every holler and hillside, branches, creeks, rivers filled with life forms, minners, tadpoles, mussels, crawdads, snake doctors, edible fish, edible frogs, clean sandy beaches along the riverbanks as late as 1955, people splashing in the swimming holes, sitting on quilts on the sand eating their picnics, resting. Now in the twenty-first century the rivers are dirty but I still pledge allegiance to them, and to all who work to get them clean again and stop the nest fouling. People are the only creatures who foul their own nests, garbage, sewage, mountaintop removal mining. Animals know better. I pledge allegiance to the animals, and to the trees, remnants of the ancient hardwood forests, ten thousand years in the making, that covered eastern America, and in one century it was all destroyed. I pledge allegiance to the old Indians who were native to this land until the Euros, my ancestors among them, destroyed them in their millions. I honor the native peoples. I honor those in the mountain region who have chronicled the history, made us know what happened, the good and the bad. And all praise to those who, across the generations, have made the poetry and music and remembered the old stories and told them in human voices. All praise to the young people who have listened and will tell the tales again and add their own. And the senior people, the older ones, with us still and those gone on, I see them in my mind, carry them in my heart, and I thank them all, and will sing their names as a song, in pledge of my allegiance.

The Photograph

MY MOTHER and her people and my father and his people had stayed up all night at Grandma and Granddad Collier's house in 1944, arguing over where I was going to live while my father was gone to war. My mother whom I hadn't seen in a year and her sisters Arnetta and Ruth and some boyfriend of Ruth's had tried to take me away to Indianapolis for the duration but my father who was home on furlough and Grandma and Granddad and Aunt Evelyn and her husband L.C. had shouted them down until finally about four o'clock in the morning my mother and her sisters and the man with them all left shrieking and crying. I was only five and in bed but wide awake, of course, listening through the walls to all that was said. I felt guilty because I knew I wanted to stay at Grandma's instead of going with my mother. I loved my mother but she was strange and Grandma's house had been my home as long as I could remember and I didn't want to go away with anyone. Even though I wanted to stay at Grandma's she said things about my mother that I dreaded to hear her say. I thought at first that the man with them was my mother's boyfriend instead of Aunt Ruth's. Grandma had been telling me that my mother ran around with nasty men and that was why I didn't see her very often, but I knew that wasn't true. She said that my mother wasn't fit to be my mother anymore. I knew that wasn't true either. I was only five but I knew how to

7

hear that kind of grownup talk without feeling anything about it one way or another. Through the walls I heard my mother crying and pleading and Aunt Ruth cussing and then Grandma and my father shouting. Then I heard some dishes smash on the floor and several doors slam including the doors of the car my mother and the people with her had come in.

The next day we took my father to the bus station in town so he could get back to his Army unit that was headed overseas. He hugged me goodbye in front of the bus station and Aunt Jenny took me by the hand and led me through the throngs of people down Main Street to the Kentucky Theater and came inside to sit with me for a few minutes, according to our custom. I felt strange from staying awake all night the night before but I was excited as always to be going to the show. I was only five but I was well able to sit in the movies by myself. Ever since my mom had moved to Indianapolis and my dad had been in the Army, Jenny had been taking me to the movies on Saturdays. She would come inside and sit with me until I was settled. Then she would pat me on the hand and steal out of the theater to shop in the stores while I watched the show.

I hardly noticed when she patted my hand this time for I was quickly lost in the newsreel images of war on the movie screen, falling bombs and burning buildings and battleships firing their huge guns as the Marines landed on the beachhead. When someone patted my arm again and whispered my name I thought it was Jenny come back to tell me something. It was too dark to see him at first but then I felt his presence, felt the mystery of my father kneeling beside me like a shadow in the aisle, his actual hand upon my actual arm. Then in the light from the screen I saw my father's sad face looking at me. Wilgus, he whispered, come outside a minute, I'll bring you right back.

We had already said goodbye yet there he was again. How could that be? Wordlessly I walked with my father up the aisle to the lobby and then to the street outside where the afternoon light was so bright I had to close my eyes. I tried to follow him through the crowd but I kept stumbling until he lifted me to his shoulders and carried me high above the throng. All the way up Main Street, past clothing stores and hardware stores and jewelry stores and drugstores, past the courthouse where two old men on the top step preached simultaneously to the crush of people below, my father carried me. Then suddenly he set me on the ground and by the hand led me through a door into a photo store where a little man I'd never seen before quickly sat me on a stool behind a curtain. With his small hands he pointed my face straight ahead. Then he stepped back and opened the curtain and then a light flashed before my eyes, so bright I was blinded again.

Then my father led me outside again, and again swung me onto his shoulders and off we went down the street again, passing rows of buses whose motors were running as soldiers lined up at their doors. Past the post office and the courthouse and the stores, through the crowd we ran the length of Main Street back to the Kentucky Theater where my father stood me on my feet again and led me by the hand down the dark aisle to the same seat I had occupied before. You be a good boy, he whispered. He pressed his cheek to the top of my head and touched my face with his hand. Then he was gone. I sat there blind a long time but gradually my eyes adjusted and several years went by. When my father died in the Veterans Hospital in 1951 and the hospital sent his belongings home in a box, I found the picture the little man took of me that day, and pictures of my mother as well.

9

Karo

GRANDMA THOUGHT our old dog Karo had gone mad. Karo was real old and she frothed around her mouth some but I knew she wasn't mad. I tried to get in on the talk about Karo but nobody listened to me. Grandma told Uncle Delmer they might have to shoot Karo. I thought it was something they'd talk about some more and I went to the front yard to play. But then I heard a gunshot and I ran back and there was Karo flopping on the ground by the coal pile, shrieking and crying and trying to pull herself along with her front legs. Delmer had shot Karo in the hindquarters with his .38 pistol. I wasn't but nine but I knew that if he had to kill her he ought to of tied her to a post and took a steady aim at her head with a .22 rifle like you would a hog. Delmer had stood on the back porch steps and tried to kill Karo with a pistol from way across the yard, and her running. Soon as I come around the house there was another shot, and then another one. The bullets hit Karo in the belly and in the neck and they still didn't kill her. She screamed and cried and tried to crawl away. Then Grandma came running out of the house with the .22, cussing Delmer all to pieces. She was going to get up close and put poor Karo out of her misery. But then Delmer shot again and this time he hit Karo in the head and she quit screaming. Delmer's last shot almost hit Grandma. She stopped in her tracks and stared at Karo on the ground. Then she walked over to Delmer and took his pistol away from him. She said, "You leave my house." Delmer looked like he didn't know who Grandma was. But he obeyed her. When he went out of sight behind the house I ran over to where Karo was laying. Her body was tore all to pieces.

"Get the shovel, Wilgus. Get the pick."

I watched Grandma open the corn crib in the barn and take out a feed sack. While I went to get the tools, Grandma wrapped Karo up in the burlap. About that time Aunt Evelyn came out of the house and walked over to where we stood. Grandma carried Karo in her arms and Evelyn helped me carry the pick and shovel and we headed out across the field.

We dug Karo's grave under the bamgilly tree in the field behind the barn. Grandma did most of the work. She fixed the burlap bag tighter around Karo, then laid her in the grave. I helped shovel the dirt back in the hole. When the work was finished, Grandma picked up a flat limestone rock and put it on the grave. Then she picked up the shovel and started walking back to the house. Aunt Evelyn walked behind Grandma, carrying the pick. I stayed at the grave awhile, glad to be alone with my dog.

Tommy Cassinelli

TOMMY CASSINELLI was a bully at school and he pushed me around some but somehow I was never afraid of him. I could take whatever push or shove or knock-down there might be. I was sorry when he made some of the smaller boys cry and run away. But still, in a strange way, Tommy felt like kinfolks to me. We lived in the same coal camp and our fathers loaded coal together in the mine, and they were both union guys. Sometimes Tommy's mother would help my mother who was tired much of the time and always kind of sad.

After school we boys would play around the pile of railroad ties next to the tracks in front of the commissary. Sometimes we played on the tracks, putting nails or pennies on the rails for the train to flatten. Sometimes we would play a game called Hobo where we would jump onto a slow-moving train and ride it as it picked up speed. This was still in the steam engine days when the train roared and sent up billows of smoke and ashes and swirling coal dust so thick you had to keep your eyes closed half the time. We clung like monkeys to the sides of the gons, sometimes hanging on to the steel stepping bars with one hand and waving to each other with the other. The cowards would jump off soon after they got on but others of us would stay on as the train went faster, and then jump off one by one when our courage ran out until finally only Tommy Cassinelli was still riding.

I wasn't any good at fighting or throwing rocks or running races, games that required agility. I was not an agile kid. But I could maintain, hold on, I could take it, tenacity was my secret power. Several times I was the last boy on the train with Tommy. One time we jumped on the same coal gon, he at the forward end and I at the back. The wind blew dust in our eyes so we could barely see and the roar of the wheels, steel on steel, was so loud it overwhelmed all other sounds. I waved at Tommy but he was looking ahead and didn't see me. I wanted him to know that it was me on the coal gon with him. I held onto the steel bar with one hand and waved like crazy, whirling my arm around and around until finally he did notice me and waved back. We looked at each other through half-closed eyes as the blurred world beside the tracks rushed by faster and faster. I knew I would jump before Tommy but something in me made me want to push him past his own limit, make him a better hobo and in the process make myself a better hobo too. Finally I let go of my bar and flew outwards and down into the weeds, then walked the mile or two on the railroad tracks back home.

In school Tommy still shoved me around a little but I could tell that now he recognized that there was a limit where I was concerned. I think we would have become real friends if there'd been more time. One day in November two men came to the school and spoke to Miss Turner and Miss Turner told Tommy to go with the men and he did and I never saw him again. His father's legs had been cut off in a mine accident that afternoon and during the night he died.

The next day the Cassinellis' camp house was empty. We never did learn where they moved to, or why they left so suddenly. It was a strange feeling. Another family soon moved into their house but they didn't stay long. That winter the mine laid off half the workers and by spring, half the houses in the camp were empty.

Sometime in the early sixties the company tore the coal camp down, but I still go out to the site from time to time. The buildings are gone, but the places, the spaces where they stood, are still there, grown up in saplings, slowly being covered by the kudzu vines.

Snow Day

I WENT TO Rock Creek School. I was in the first grade. During recess it come a big snow. Miss Keck said for us to all get home quick before it got too deep to walk. On the way up Trace Fork me and Randall and Clifton got to throwing snowballs at one another. We didn't have any gloves on. The snow was two or three inches deep by then and still falling. I scooped up a bunch of snow and packed it into a snowball. I felt a sting in my left hand and then there was blood all over my snowball. A piece of glass was in the snow and it cut my hand. I stood in the road looking at my hand and at my blood dripping on the snow. I yelled out to Randall and Clifton that I had cut my hand. They ran over to see. Then we all took off running up the road.

I lived in the furthest-up house so I walked the last part by myself. There wasn't any cars coming and no other people outdoors but me. Everything was real quiet. I stood still and looked around at the world. The trees had snow on them. I heard the snow pecking on the leaves. There was snow on the creek banks and on the rocks in the middle of the creek. Snowflakes filled the whole air around me. I breathed them in my nose. The wind was blowing some but I didn't feel cold. I watched my blood make red splashes on the snow. I held my hand out and turned around and around to make it drip in a circle. Pretty quick the red disappeared under new snow.

Up the hill I could see the corner of Grandma's house through the trees. I decided to get off the road and walk straight uphill through the trees to the house. There was holly trees and hazel bushes and laurel dells and mistletoe on the oak trees with snow over it all. There was a big rock on the hillside that had a ledge sticking out for a shelter. I got back in under there and squatted down and looked out. Maybe I could build a fire and cook some meat over it. Maybe I could live there. I didn't want to leave but I was cold and had to get on home.

When I come out from under the ledge there was a soldier in a red uniform standing among the trees. He had a tall red hat on and a red cape and black boots and a sword at his side. He looked me in the eye. Then he reached around and took his cape off and wrapped it around my shoulders. A little while later I woke up under my own quilts in my bed. Grandma felt of my forehead. She asked me if I was warm. I was toasty warm. I wanted to go back to sleep and sleep a long time more.

Delmer's Scalp Wound

UNCLE DELMER came home from the mine with blood all over his head, running across his face and down his neck. He'd been operating a drill in the mine, getting ready to set a charge, when his hair got caught in the drill bit. It pulled out a chunk of his scalp big as his hand. Delmer wouldn't let anybody take him to the hospital. He drove himself home twelve miles in Junior's Ford. He wouldn't let anybody at the house help him either. Jenny and Evelyn were both there, and Grandma, but he wouldn't let anybody touch him. "Leave me alone," he said. He held up both hands to protect himself. He went in the wash house and took a shower bath and put on clean clothes. Then he wrapped a white towel around his head and drove himself to the hospital in town. At the hospital they put him under ether and operated on his head. When he woke up he wouldn't stay in the hospital. Delmer told me later that he didn't stay in the hospital because he thought that under the ether he had said all sorts of stuff to the doctors and nurses that he was ashamed of. A nurse that was there named Bonnie told him all about it when he woke up. Delmer told me he said things that might even could get him killed. He came home and stayed all night, then the next day went to Chicago on the train. A few days after he went to Chicago we got a postcard from him that said he wouldn't be home for a while. But then, early in the morning three days later,

Granddad and Uncle Junior went out to the work truck to go to work. When they opened the door there was Delmer, still in his dress clothes, sound asleep on the seat. Junior said Delmer didn't change clothes or anything, he just went on back to the mine in his dress clothes like he hadn't been gone at all.

Tracking Rabbits

IN THE WINTER there was a big snow on the ground. Grand-dad asked me if I wanted to go to the pasture with him and Karo to track rabbits. I was glad to go outside. We'd been cooped up in the house for days, keeping warm by the fires in the grates and the coal stove in the kitchen. It was Christmas time and school was out. I put on my new Mackinaw coat and my toboggan and my gloves. Granddad and Karo were waiting for me at the hog pen behind the barn.

It felt funny, seeing the hog pen empty. We'd raised two big hogs that year. I'd helped feed them all summer and fall and they were big and fat. Sometimes Granddad let me feed them a pan of egg-size coal. Granddad said coal was made from plants that hogs could taste. He said it took a million years for the plants to turn into coal. Our hogs were only a year or two old. The hogs ate the coal and we ate the hogs. Hams. Sausage. Pork rinds. Souse meat from the head. Grandma kept one ham in the smokehouse for us to eat the next Fourth of July.

We had slaughtered the hogs back in December. Grandma and Granddad had a big fight on slaughtering day. Granddad always killed the hogs by hitting them in the forehead with the blunt of an axe. He would hold the hog's head between his legs and some-one else would hold it from behind. I saw him raise the axe high

21

over his head and swing it down. Somehow he hit the hog wrong and didn't stun it enough for anybody to cut its throat. The hog squealed and squealed and got loose and ran all over the barnyard and out among the fodder shocks in the field.

A man named Hagan that worked for us on hog killing day finally got a rope around its neck and Granddad helped him hold it until Grandma got there with the .22 and shot it between its eyes. The hog was too far from the barn to hoist up with the block and tackle. Granddad had to hitch the mule to the sled and haul the hog back close enough to hoist so it could bleed out, and this took time to do. Grandma said, this meat's rurnt. Granddad said it wasn't, that this was good meat. They finally got the hog hung upside down. Hagan cut its throat so the blood would drain out. Many hogs had been hung in that same place, their blood falling into the same spot on the ground.

Me and Granddad walked on up the hill real quiet in the snow. We walked past the cistern and into the woods and pretty quick saw rabbit tracks in the snow. We followed the tracks in the direction of the new ground. Karo was real excited. She had her nose in the snow almost. All at once she took off running. The rabbit's tracks led straight to a hollow log. Karo guarded one end of the log while Granddad packed the other end with snow. I helped him pack snow into the log on Karo's end. The rabbit was so quiet inside the log I wasn't sure it was in there. I thought, it must be dark in there and cold.

Granddad started chopping a hole in the middle of the log. Wood chips flew out on the snow. Granddad chopped a hole in the log big enough for him to reach in with a stick and poke around until he found where the rabbit was. Then he packed snow into the log enough to make a barrier inside. Granddad moved to the center of the end of the log where the rabbit was and started chopping again. Pretty quick he had a hole big enough to reach his arm back in. He felt around and then I heard the rabbit's high-pitched squeal as Granddad brought the rabbit out. It was brown and white with big brown eyes. Granddad held it up for me to see. Then he hit it in the back of the head with the blunt of the axe and the rabbit quit squealing and jerking around. Karo was going crazy, barking and jumping around. Finally Granddad dropped the dead rabbit to the ground and Karo grabbed it and carried it off into the trees.

The Wreck

ONE DAY the summer I turned eleven, me and my Uncle Junior went out riding in his old '36 Chevrolet. Junior was working in Cincinnati at the time. He had been a miner when he lived in Kentucky, but after the strike of '49 he pulled out and moved to Ohio to work. He eventually bought a house and settled up there, but like most of the mountain people who moved up north in those years, he came down home every weekend, nearly.

And this one time he came home in a Chevrolet he bought for a hundred dollars. He came in late on Friday night. After sleeping late and then sitting around the house all morning talking to Grandma and Granddad, Junior asked me to go for a ride with him in his new car. I was restless and glad to get to go somewhere. We took off down Trace Fork to the highway, then headed toward the county seat where Junior said he'd buy me a hamburger.

After we'd driven a few miles Junior said, "Take the wheel, Wilgus. Slide over here and drive awhile." I'd never driven a car before in my life and starting to learn was not among the things I particularly wanted to do that day. But there wasn't any way to turn down Junior's offer. I knew what he was doing and what my response had to be. My father, Junior's brother Glen, had died not long before. Junior wanted to be good to me, pay attention to me, make me feel more grown up than I was. So, I got behind the wheel and Junior took his place beside me, and with a good deal of jerking and jumping and stalling of the motor and grinding of the gears, I managed to get the Chevrolet rolling.

The road along the North Fork of the Kentucky River is twisty as a snake in Finley County, and even on Saturday there are lots of coal trucks on it. I was scared of those big trucks but Junior told me to not pay any attention to them. "Ignore 'em," he said. "Roll this thing."

So I drove along four or five miles. I was starting to feel like I had the hang of it pretty good until we came up behind an old man driving a horse pulling a wagon along the road about two miles an hour. For some reason I didn't think to put the brakes on. I just steered over into the other lane to go around him, and sure enough, a big truck loaded down with coal was coming right toward us. There was only one thing to do that would save our lives, and Junior did it. He grabbed the steering wheel and headed us across the left lane, over the road bank and across the river bottom toward the river itself. We would have gone right on into the river if Junior hadn't jerked the wheel again. He was sitting on top of me by now, cussing and praying and yelling and fighting that steering wheel. He gave it a turn and the wheels dug into the soft sandy soil of the river bottom. The car rolled onto its side and braced up against a clump of sycamore trees at the very edge of the water.

Junior was crying and yelling and carrying on so bad I thought he was killed or something. But it turned out that he wasn't hurt at all. The reason he was carrying on so was because he thought I was killed. I told him I was all right. I had a cut on my forehead that was bleeding a little, but after we held a handkerchief against it awhile, it stopped. That pacified Junior some, but he was still pretty upset. He was thinking about what Grandma would say when he took me home with a bruised head and blood all over my shirt front.

26

So me and Junior cooked up a scheme. It involved telling about a dozen lies which hurt my Christian conscience, but in the same spirit in which I'd been willing to try to drive for Junior's sake, I was willing to lie for him too. The plan was for us to hitchhike on into Blaine and buy me a new blue pullover shirt like the one I had on. Then we'd go to Randall Couch's used car lot at the edge of town and buy another hundred-dollar car. Junior would drive the car home and tell Grandma he'd traded his Chevrolet in on a better car. I would get out at the mouth of the creek and walk home, and when Grandma asked me how I cut my head I'd say in a rock fight with a bunch of mean boys from Second Creek.

Aunt Jenny and Aunt Evelyn were suspicious of our tale when we told them, but Grandma believed it absolutely. She was proud of me for standing up to the Second Creek boys. She was proud to ride to church the next day in her son's new car and doubly-proud when Junior came into the church for the service for the first time since the War. As far as I know, Grandma never did learn the truth about the wreck. The corpse of Junior's old Chevrolet lay on the river bank for years, until the '57 flood finally came and carried it away.

At the River

WE HAD GONE to Middle Fork River to go in swimming at a hole there out from Hilton by the highway bridge. A big bunch of us had ridden over in the back of my uncle Junior's new ten-ton Ford truck. This was in the days when Granddad and Uncle Junior and Uncle Delmer operated their pony mine on Puckett Creek. That mine only lasted a few years but in that time extra money circled around in our family and we could afford to have a truck.

For this outing at the river Junior had hosed out the truck bed and thrown in some hay bales for people to sit on. Grandma and Granddad rode in front with Junior but Aunt Jenny and me, Aunt Evelyn and her husband L.C., plus Delmer and his new wife Pauline and some of Pauline's people all rode in the back. Pauline's sister Maxine was one of several new in-laws we'd been getting to know since Delmer had started courting Pauline. Maxine was about twenty-five. I was thirteen. I didn't know this about her at the time but Maxine had already been married and divorced and had a little girl named Cindy who lived half the time in Middletown, Ohio, with her father.

At the river, there was a nice sandy beach and plenty of woods nearby for people to go back in and change into their swimming suits. I helped Junior and Delmer carry the quilts and the watermelons and picnic stuff down to the beach while everybody else went back in the trees to put their swimming suits on. When I went back to change I thought I was the only one there until I came upon Maxine standing next to a sycamore tree without a stitch on. I started to turn around and run but she saw me and busted out laughing. Without haste or any sign of embarrassment, Maxine stepped behind the tree where I heard her still laughing.

A minute or two later Maxine came out from behind the sycamore wearing a blue one-piece bathing suit. Carrying her clothes in one hand and her shoes and a towel in the other, and with a big grin on her face, she walked right toward me.

"I guess you got you a big eyeful that time," she sang out cheerfully. Then she said, "I won't tell anybody if you won't!"

When she got up close she gave me a push and said, "Come on, buddy, let's go in swimming," and the two of us took off running barefoot toward the river.

Chivaree

GRANDMA SAID let's go somewhere, Wilgus. We walked down the hill to the county pike and across the little bridge over Cane Creek to the Old Road and a ways further on until we came to the Cooks' house where some people were standing around in the yard. I'd been there before. The Cooks had an apple orchard and every year we bought apples from them. There was still light in the sky when we got there. Several other people were already there. Uh oh, I thought, somebody has died. More people walked into the Cooks' front yard and over to a little guest house out from the Cooks' dwelling house toward the barn. It had pawpaw trees on either side of it and a chopping block I had hid behind one time playing whoopy hide with the Cook kids. Pretty soon it was dark. Everybody got real quiet. Then a big racket broke out around the little guest house. Somebody shot fire crackers. Others blew whistles and rang cowbells and banged on pots and pans. *Come out!* the people yelled. Grown up people. *Come out of there!* Whooping and banging and yelling. Finally a young man and woman opened the door and stepped out onto the little porch and everybody cheered the newlyweds. It was my first chivaree.

I Killed My Pony

AFTER THE WAR my uncles went in the coal business with Granddad. They opened a pony mine in the number four seam on Puckett Creek. They brought the coal out in one-ton mining cars pulled by brownish gray work ponies. One pony was red. Granddad said Red was my pony. I loved Red. I fed him corn from my hand sometimes. He liked carrots too. After supper everybody rested under the maple tree in the front yard. I tied a rope around Red's neck and brought him from the barn and tied him to a low limb of the tree so he could pick the green grass. At dark we all went to bed. I forgot about Red. The next morning I went out to the yard and Red was dead. He had walked around the tree until the rope bound his head to the trunk. Then he fell and hung himself. I killed my pony.

For Every Antidote

ONE TIME WHEN I was in high school and still living with my grandparents, some neighbors down the creek burned a big pile of trash in their backyard that had about three years' accumulation of family junk in it. These particular neighbors did a lot of hunting and trapping and hide-processing at their place, so inevitably there were various kinds of animal scraps, hides and feathers in the pile. They burned several old mattresses, a couple of stuffed chairs, an old couch and about a dozen worn-out tires in this fire, sending a column of oily black smoke rising above the trees where it billowed into a ball, then spread up and down Trace Fork to hover above us all like a shroud.

My Uncle Delmer was living in his trailer at the time, a little one-room camper affair that he kept parked on the creek bank about halfway between Grandma's house and our trash-burning neighbors. He was still married to Pauline but they fought so much that Delmer would retreat to his little house, which Pauline called his "drinking and pouting house."

Delmer had come home from the war a very heavy drinker, but he was never officially an alcoholic. In later years some would have labeled him a "binge drinker." Sometimes he'd go a whole year and never touch a drop. Then something would go wrong in his life and he would go back to his regular drinking habits.

It so happened that when the neighbors lit their trash fire, Delmer was in the middle of what turned out to be a five-week drunk. This was when his natural paranoid tendencies would start to show. And as we all know, paranoia sometimes brings with it an inflated sense of personal grandeur. As the dark smoke swirled around his trailer, Delmer was certain that it was poison gas, aimed at him personally by his enemies.

As confused as Delmer could get from time to time, he was still a very clever man. When the neighbors fired up their trash pile, most of the folks on the creek simply shut their doors and windows and waited for the smoke to go away on its own. Delmer closed the trailer's one window but he had more aggressive ideas for his one door. From a shed out back Delmer dragged in a very large floor fan and mounted it in the smallish door of his trailer to blow outward against the poison gas. Heedless of the mounting electric bill, Delmer let his fan run day and night for three days. When the last odor from the fire finally left the hollow, he unplugged his fan, opened a beer for himself and one for me, and together we drank to his victory.

After his fourth beer Delmer said, "I guess we kicked their ass that time, didn't we buddy?"

"Damn right," I said cheerily. We clicked our bottles together and then opened two more.

"Wilgus, I know you're a grown man, but you're still young. There's something you need to understand."

"What about?" I asked.

"About life. Surviving. Getting through this world."

"I'm always ready to learn, Delmer. Tell me."

"Just don't ever forget that the enemy is full of tricks that can throw you off, but you can still beat him."

"How?" I asked.

"Keep a clear mind," Delmer said, "and remember that for every antidote, there's a dote."

Linville Price

THERE USED TO BE this old boy on our creek named Linville Price who was known for his eccentric and sometimes shady dealings with people. He wasn't dishonest exactly but Linville didn't always tell the truth either. One time during one of his stints as operator of a roadside country grocery store he pointed to a chocolate cake that had been sitting on his bread shelf for a couple of days and told me that my grandmother had ordered that cake especially and that it would be a favor to him and her both if I would carry it home to Grandma. We agreed that it made sense for me to go ahead and pay Linville the three dollars right then, and Grandma would reimburse me.

When I got home I quickly learned that Grandma had certainly not ordered any cake from Linville Price. But she didn't make me take it back. It was too dry to eat so she just threw it in the slop bucket, gave me three dollars and said she'd deal with Linville later on. I'm pretty sure she never mentioned it to him. Like a lot of people, Grandma had a soft spot in her heart for ol' Linville. He was well into his middle age but there was something boyish about him. He was charming the way certain good traders are charming, yet pitiful, too, as if he needed protection from the rougher edges of life.

In addition to his little grocery stores, none of which ever lasted more than a year, Linville's entrepreneurial spirit occasionally inspired him to open his own auto repair shop, Linville's Garage he always called it. He was a fair jackleg automobile mechanic when he set his mind to it, and every time he'd go back in the car repair business people always brought their cars to him. Linville's garages always came to the same end as his grocery stores but usually not in time to save me from yet another strange and costly encounter with him.

One time when I'd just come back from one of my trips to Chicago, Linville told me he thought he heard a knocking in the motor of my Ford. Seemed like I needed a valve job. Take him two days, three at most, to get it done. I was on the road quite a bit that year and needed a reliable car so I said okay. Linville took the head off the engine that very first day but the next day he had to go to Hazard to help his cousin Roger put underpinning around his ex-wife Jewel Dean's trailer and didn't get back for three days. Another hour under the hood of my car revealed that my motor needed parts that Linville didn't have and that he'd have to call a parts store in Lexington and have what we needed sent up on the Greyhound bus.

Well, as I should have expected, ten days went by and my Ford's engine remained in scattered pieces amid the general clutter of Linville's garage floor. When Linville got arrested for hauling liquor across a county line, I wound up having to hire Roger to come over from Perry County and finish the valve job on my Ford.

Everybody knew part of what Linville did for a living but nobody knew everything he did, or understood how whatever it was he did do added up to a livelihood. Sometimes you'd see Linville working with a carpenter crew around the county for a few weeks, helping somebody build a barn or a house or overhaul a store front, but then for a month you wouldn't see him at all. Occasionally on

Saturdays you could find him at the Whitaker Stock Sale peddling some item or other, or perhaps helping a friend or relative operate their booth at the flea market.

One time at one of the sales I came across Linville standing next to a pickup truck loaded down with used automobile tires. This was in the late 1960s and I was driving my new Volkswagen by then. Linville said, "Wilgus, let me sell you a set of good tires."

I said, "Linville, I've got a new car, I won't need any tires for two or three years I hope."

"Well," he said, "you never can tell. You never know when you'd be very glad you had some backup tires like these. I can let you have four for five dollars apiece, that's just twenty dollars, Wilgus. It'd be worth twenty dollars just for that good, secure feeling."

When it became clear to Linville that I wasn't going to buy any of his tires that day he deftly said, "Well, get you a pack of these flashlights instead, four flashlights for just nine dollars, and if you get two packs they're a dollar off each, that'd just be sixteen dollars. That's a bargain if I ever seen one, Wilgus. The time'll come when you'll be glad you bought these flashlights."

"Why don't you sell me one flashlight for two dollars, Linville. I might could use one flashlight."

"All right," he said, "that's a deal, and you know what? Just to be fair, I'm going to flat-out just give you one of these good 13-inch tires here. A man ought to have extra tires, Wilgus, I'll worry about you if you don't take it."

"Whatever," I said, and as I shelled out the two dollars for the flashlight he said, "Wilgus, it being you, for just three dollars more, I'll let you have another of these tires. That'll give you a pair, two good tires for three dollars, you can't beat that."

"Fine," I said, and peeled off three more ones for the second tire.

When I got home that evening I looked closely at the tires for the first time. Both of them had breaks in the inner lining and were totally useless. Naturally this made me think I ought to check my new flashlight too. The thing was so rusty inside I couldn't even get the bulb-end unscrewed.

I was furious enough to choke Linville after the tires and flashlight episode, but a few days later he demonstrated that peculiar quality he possessed that endeared him even to his victims and protected him from the wrath of the world he moved through so adroitly.

For the first time in several months all my aunts and uncles came home for the weekend. In the old days our big family would gather at the homeplace every weekend nearly, but as time had gone by we came to feel lucky if we all made it home at the same time once a year. I hadn't seen Aunt Jenny in six months and I was shocked by how sick she looked. She'd lost a lot of weight and was pale as a ghost. She was so weak I wondered how she had driven a car all the way from North Carolina by herself. After supper on Saturday evening, several of us were sitting around the kitchen table, talking, when all of a sudden a big gush of blood spurted out of Jenny's mouth. Before anybody could move to catch her, she fell to the floor right in the middle of her own blood. Everybody started screaming and carrying on so bad I thought sure Jenny was dead.

"Call the ambulance!" Grandma yelled, but Uncle Junior and Uncle Delmer had already picked Jenny up to carry her out to Junior's station wagon. At the hospital, me and Junior and Delmer each gave Jenny a pint of blood, but the doctor said she had to have immediate surgery for a bleeding stomach ulcer and would need at least ten more pints during the night.

A little before midnight a nurse handed me the Finley County phone book and told me to start calling people to come in and donate some blood to the hospital. I must have called twenty people all over the county to ask if they'd be willing to come to the hospital and contribute blood, but not one was able or willing to do it. I was still on the phone at two o'clock in the morning when who should walk by the phone desk in the lobby but Linville Price.

Linville had come to the hospital to visit a brother-in-law who'd accidentally shot himself in the calf with a .22 pistol a few hours before. "What's going on?" he asked me. As soon as I told him about Jenny and the need for blood, Linville said, "How much do you need?" and started rolling up his sleeve.

I said, "The hospital will take any kind you got." It turned out that Linville's blood type matched Jenny's and within the hour his very blood was flowing into my aunt's veins.

But I still needed nine more pints. I mumbled some words to the effect that I'd go out and buy some damn blood if I knew anybody that was selling it. Why was I not surprised when ol' Linville looked me in the eye and said, "How much would you pay?"

"Ten dollars a pint," I said, pulling a figure out of the air, ninety dollars cash right then and there for nine pints of blood.

Linville said, "Get your money ready," and with no more words than that he turned around and went back out the hospital entrance still without having visited his wounded brother-in-law.

Forty-five minutes later Linville was back again, this time with a badge on his chest and a .38 pistol in a holster strapped to his hip and nine prisoners from the county jail marching behind him like a row of ducks. It turned out that Linville was friends with and probably kin to both the jailer and the sheriff. From the jail he had called the sheriff and gotten himself deputized over the telephone. Then he'd gone into the cell block and asked the prisoners if any of them would like to go out in town for a few hours, take a nice

43

walk in the fresh air to the hospital, get a free glass of orange juice plus a free pack of cigarettes and a piece of good pie, in return for donating a pint of blood on behalf of a woman on the operating table that might die if they didn't do it. Twenty prisoners volunteered immediately and it took the jailer a few minutes to select the most worthy donors. Soon, all were marching proudly through the hospital lobby down a hall to the lab where each man did his duty.

"I've been in jail," Linville said to me as I handed him his ninety dollars. I offered him ten dollars more for his own pint of blood but he wouldn't take it. He said, "I know what jailbirds want. They want out, even if only for a little while. They want cigarettes too. Have you ever been in jail, Wilgus?" I said no. But years later, when in fact I did spend a night in the very jail from whence came the blood that saved my aunt, I thought kindly about Linville. He's been dead for years by now, but a lot of people up around home remember him with affection, myself among them.

The Dance

ONE MORNING about a month before he died, Granddad Collier and I were in the living room at the homeplace watching TV together. It was unusual for Granddad to watch TV at all, let alone that early in the morning. But he'd been sick for several months, he hadn't been able to go outside very much. This was the first time he'd come out of his bedroom fully clothed in several days. I was drinking coffee and flipping through some old magazines and only half-watching the television. I closed my magazine and turned the volume up, and the two of us settled in our chairs to watch the *Today* show.

The show had the usual news and weather reports and advertising and chit-chat among the announcers. But finally they got around to the feature part of the program, which that morning was a five-minute excerpt from a new film about village life in modern China. This was in the days when film reports from China were exceedingly rare, especially on American television. This one had been made by a British crew that had been given access to one of the model agricultural communes. There were pictures of smiling Chinese people working in the fields, of small children singing in school, of people going down a dirt road on bicycles. Granddad watched these scenes with moderate interest.

But when the film cut to pictures of a group of elderly Chinese men taking their exercise in a courtyard, Granddad's interest really

45

came alive. He leaned forward in his chair and turned the sound up, then stayed forward with his face close to the screen. The old Chinese men looked right back at him, unsmiling. Their bodies moved in graceful unison through a routine that seemed to be a form of Tai Chi. Stretching and turning, bending and posing, the old men moved with profound elegance through the series of gestures and poses. They were truly old men, the community elders. Naked to the waist, their bodies were thin as the bodies of small boys. These men had lived long and seen much, and yet, their old faces had a strangely youthful aspect to them. They seemed relaxed and untroubled. The morning sun was shining on them. It was as if the sun was feeding them directly, making their bodies fluid, flexible, full of strength and grace.

After a while Granddad got up and went on back to his room and I didn't see him again until the early afternoon. It was a day in early spring in Kentucky, when the mornings are overcast and cold, but when the afternoons are sunny and warm enough to go outside in your shirtsleeves. We had been having sunny afternoons for several days but so far my grandfather hadn't felt like going out into them. This particular day, however, about an hour after eating a bowl of soup in his room for lunch, Granddad put on his sweater and coat and went outside to stand in the sun alone. Then, slowly, he raised his arms above his head and stretched himself real good. He bent to one side, then the other, keeping his arms outstretched.

Granddad stretched and turned, he bent and lowered his arms all in a flowing motion that became a dance as he kept it up. Herschel Collier, my grandfather, ex-logger, retired coal miner, hillside farmer, age eighty-three, was standing beside his house in the Kentucky mountains, in the sunshine of one of the last spring days of his life, doing the Kentucky version of Tai Chi.

Granddad danced for several minutes before he heard the screen door slam on the far side of the house. Someone was coming. Quickly he stuffed his hands back in his coat pockets and resumed his slow walk around the yard. As far as I know, he never did Tai Chi in the sun again.

Fifteen Dollars

ON ONE of my last visits with Aunt Jenny in the nursing home, she said, "Wilgus, when you were little, did anybody tell you much about your great-granddaddy, old Electious Whitt?"

"I know he owned the whole head of Trace Fork at one time," I said.

"Did anybody tell you much about his wife Opal that died?"

I actually knew a great deal about Opal and Electious. Most of what I knew about them had come from Jenny herself in my growing-up years. But she was into storytelling now so when she asked me if I remembered much about them, I lied and said not much.

Jenny sipped from her plastic tumbler and then leaned back against the pillows on her bed. "I'll tell you, that Opal was the dearest little woman that ever was. She was my grandmother, you see, my mother's mother, which makes Opal and Electious your great-grandmother and father. I wish you could have known her, Wilgus. Everybody that knew Opal loved her. I was just a little girl in the last years of her life, but I loved her to pieces. She was a very sweet and dedicated Christian woman. She was saintly, so good-hearted and generous, and hard working too. She wasn't big as a minute but she could work from daylight 'til dark and never slow down. And it was real work too. You've seen how my mother worked, what all she could do. Opal was just like that. If you want

49

to know where your grandma learned how to work, it was from her mother Opal. She was a wonderful mother. She bore Electious eight children that lived and every one of them turned out pretty good if I say so myself."

"She sounds like a real strong person."

"Yes. But the thing was, people thought Opal was so enduring, it didn't occur to any of us that her health could go bad. But all of a sudden, in 1922, she came down with the heart dropsy and in just a few weeks she died. She was fifty-three years old."

"That's my age now," I said.

"Honey, you're young. Opal was young. It tore us all to pieces when she died. It about killed Granddaddy. For months after Opal's funeral, it was like he didn't care if he lived or died. He got so he wouldn't do a thing for himself hardly. He wouldn't even eat if somebody didn't hand him a plate of food. All he wanted to do was sit on the porch of their old house and stare out at the world."

"That's a sad picture."

"It was. It was like when Opal died he wanted to die, too, and go be with her. It was all the family could do to keep him from going right on to glory. I was just a little thing when all this happened, eight years old, but I remember it well. I remember my mother being awful worried about her daddy. She and some of her sisters and brothers tried to look after him, help maintain the place, keep the weeds cut back and fix a few things. But they couldn't keep the old home place up the way Opal had. That house and yard pert near went to seed. It got to be the most lonesome place in the world up there."

Jenny paused to clear her throat. I picked up her water cup and offered it to her but she waved it away. She pointed to the Kleenex box on the table by her bed and I handed it to her. When she had wiped her lips with a tissue she set the box on her lap and resumed talking.

50

"Since we lived the closest to Granddaddy, Mommy and us kids saw him every day. Every day Mommy would fix a dinner for Electious and one of us young'uns would carry it up to him. There was a haul road up there but we always took the path through the woods, it didn't take but a few minutes to get there. I was just eight but I was plenty big enough to carry somebody a plate of food. In the evenings Mommy would take him his supper and sit with him awhile, and then carry the dishes back down with her. Electious had very little to say to anybody during that time. Once a week or so, he'd come down to our house and eat supper with us. He still wouldn't say much but he seemed to enjoy sitting on the porch watching us kids play. We always tried to get him to stay all night with us, but he never would. And he wouldn't let any of us stay at his house, neither. It was like, after Opal died, he took on a whole other personality.

"So, this arrangement went on for awhile. Then one evening, late in the summer, Mommy took Granddaddy's supper up to him as usual, and as usual I tagged along with her. To our great surprise, we found a strange woman we never had seen before, sitting out on the porch with Electious. She was tall and bony-looking. She had reddish-looking hair that she kept drawn back behind her head in a bun. Her and Granddaddy were sitting in rocking chairs with Bibles open in their laps. Come to find out, she was a church lady from across the mountain, way down on Bonnet Creek somewhere. She'd been to see Granddaddy several times, to have prayer with him, is what they said. She was a widow woman named Tildy something or other. We found out she'd been bringing food to Granddaddy too."

Jenny glanced down at her hands. When she looked up I thought I saw a trace of a smile on her lips.

"So what do you think Mommy thought about this situation, Wilgus?"

"I'd say she was quite suspicious of this widow woman," I said.

"Mommy was furious at her. But when she tried to talk to Granddaddy about it, he blowed up on her. He got mad as fire at Mommy, cussed her out and told her to go away and never come back. Talk about hurting somebody's feelings. Mommy cried for a week after that. But there wasn't anything to do. For awhile, we just quit going up there. After about a month, you talk about a shock. Word came that Granddaddy had walked across the mountain and married that woman, without telling a soul on Trace Fork about it. And to top it off, he brought her back to the homeplace to live, right there in the house that him and Opal had built with their own hands, lived in all those years, and raised us young'uns. Old bitch. Can you imagine? After Mommy nursing him when Opal died, taking care of him, carrying him food, keeping the home place up, then him turning against her like that? It was like Granddaddy had gone crazy. It was awful."

I could tell Jenny was getting tired. She closed her eyes and for a moment seemed to be sleeping. When she opened them again she motioned for me to rearrange her pillows for her. I fluffed them and helped her sit up straight again.

"Aye Lord, Wilgus, life sure is strange. It's so full of surprises. Within a month, Granddaddy was miserable with that old Tildy. He hated her, hated living with her, hated looking at her little old pinched-in face, hated how she talked. That woman turned out to be the meanest, most selfish, ignorant thing that ever was, and lazy on top of that. Wouldn't turn her hand to save herself. Wouldn't cook. She mistreated Granddaddy something awful. She got him so depressed he couldn't raise his head. You can bet this

52

development changed his tune toward my mother, all right. One afternoon Electious came walking down to our house and begged Mommy to do something to get him out of his mess.

"Mommy told him she'd think on it. Actually, soon as Granddaddy left, she busted out laughing. She'd already figured out that Electious was miserable and that something had to be done about the situation. She let a few days go by, I think to punish Granddaddy for hurting her feelings so bad. But then, one afternoon, right in the middle of a bean-stringing, Mommy stood up, took her apron off, went in the house and came back out carrying her black pocket book. 'I'm going up there,' she said, and headed up the path to the homeplace. Naturally I trotted right along behind her.

"When we got to the house, Tildy was sitting on the front porch in a rocking chair, sound asleep in broad daylight. When Mommy stepped onto the porch Tildy jumped up out of her chair and said, 'What in the world?'

"Mommy said, 'Tildy! I don't like how you treat my daddy. You're mean as a snake and nobody around here likes you. Daddy's about to kick you out of here, but I don't want you pestering him about it, or making a fuss or upsetting him any more than you already have. So if you'll leave here right now, this very minute, I'll give you fifteen dollars!'

"Tildy stood there bug-eyed as Mommy reached in her pocket book and took out three five-dollar bills and waved them in Tildy's face. It shocked Tildy to death. She fluttered and spluttered and stammered and jerked around like she was having a fit.

"Mommy said, 'And if you don't take this money and leave here, I'll whip you off this mountain with a hickory switch. I'll beat you with my fists. I'll make you sorry you ever laid eyes on my daddy.' Tildy glared at Mommy like she wanted to fight. Mommy stared right back at her. Finally Tildy grabbed that money out of Mommy's hand and set out around the hill as fast as she could go. And that was the last that anybody on Trace Fork ever seen or heard tell of Tildy.

"A few days after she left, come to find out, she wasn't any church woman after all, and she wasn't from Bonnet Creek, neither. She had come over there from Owsley County to do housework for a family. And listen to this: there never was any proof that her and Granddaddy were legally married. Nobody ever bothered him about it, never mentioned it to him. Mommy said to just let it go and be glad Electious was back to his old self. Granddaddy lived a good many more years after that. And he's up there on that mountain right now, laying in the ground next to Opal."

Uncle Jake's Grave

By THE TIME Aunt Jenny moved into the nursing home in Winchester, I was one of the few family members left to go visit her. I usually traveled to Lexington two or three times a month in the normal course of things so it was easy to stop in at the nursing home and visit Jenny awhile. Sometimes I would take her out in the car and drive her around the country roads for a couple of hours. Once or twice a year I would set aside a whole day and take her on a drive back to Finley County in the hills to visit people and places that were familiar to her from the old days.

There had been a time, years ago, when you couldn't count all the members of our big family in Finley County. But as the years passed, most of the people Jenny had known from her generation had either died or moved away. Her favorite places to visit were the little family cemeteries scattered in the coves and hollows of Finley County. Some of the cemeteries were so remote, and so many of the old-time people were gone, that they weren't maintained anymore. Over the years the roads leading to some of them became so overgrown by saplings and kudzu vines, you couldn't get a regular automobile up to them.

The most important cemetery, of course, was on our family's old homeplace on Trace Fork where she had grown up and where her own grandparents and mother and father and brothers and sisters all lay buried. Jenny's parents were Grandma and Granddad to me. Since I'd grown up in their house, her sisters and brothers had been like my own big sisters and brothers except for Jenny's oldest brother Glen, who was my father.

Another important cemetery to Jenny was the Dalton family's, on Hanks Branch in Owsley County. Jenny's Uncle Jake had married Truetta Dalton and lived with her for forty-seven years there in Owsley County. After the head of Hanks Branch was strip mined in the late 1970s, you needed a four-wheel drive vehicle to get past the mud and rocks and uprooted trees that had slid down the hill from the strip mine above. Finally visitors had to leave their vehicle and walk the last fifty yards to the cemetery. It was a major exertion for Jenny to negotiate the broken ground but she was always determined to get to that cemetery.

Up in the corner of the cemetery there was a big grave stone that Uncle Jake, who was Jenny's mother's brother and therefore my great-uncle, had put up when his wife Truetta died in the late 1960s. Jake had Truetta's name and birth date and death date chiseled into the stone. Next to it was his own name and birth date. The space for his death date was empty, to be filled in someday. This seemed fitting to the Collier family, for Uncle Jake and Aunt Truetta had been married and reportedly quite happy together for over forty years. They had raised a big family and some of their children were already buried near their mother. We all took it for granted that Uncle Jake would be placed there next to Aunt Truetta someday.

But then an unforeseen thing happened. I remember folks in our family being surprised when a year or so after Truetta died, Uncle Jake started making trips to Middlesboro about once a month. We were puzzled when he started making those trips once a week, and downright shocked when Jake at the age of seventy-three wound up married in Middlesboro to a widow by the name of Lula Flowers.

It was hard for the older folks in our family to get used to Uncle Jake being married again, but after some time had gone by we all decided we liked Lula well enough. Eventually Jake and Lula moved to Kingsport and later to Maryville, Tennessee. In all their moving about, and after Grandma and Granddad died, our side of the family quit hearing from Uncle Jake. Years went by and no letters or phone calls came and finally we realized that we had lost touch with Uncle Jake completely.

I offered to drive Jenny to Maryville to see if we could find Jake but she didn't want to go. Let him be, she said. He's probably busy. She didn't need to see him but it was important to Jenny to know if her uncle was still alive because he was the last one left in her family who was older than her. She didn't talk much about it but it was clear she wanted and perhaps needed to have some blood kin somewhere who was senior to her. I hadn't known this but Jenny remembered that one of the famous details about Jake and Lula people gossiped about had been their agreement that when they died, they wanted to be buried by their first spouses. So Aunt Jenny's way of finding out if Uncle Jake was alive or dead was to go to the cemetery every year to see if his death date had been chiseled into the stone.

Let's go check on Jake, Jenny would say matter-of-factly as we neared the time of our annual expedition, and off we would go to look at Jake's gravestone. Every year Jenny would see with her own eyes that the space for his death date remained uninscribed. One more time she would come away feeling good that she wasn't the oldest one left alive in her family. Well, it happened that one time after one of our visits to the family cemetery, Jenny and I stopped to get gas and buy some soft drinks at a service station on the Rock Creek Road, two or three miles from the mouth of Hanks Branch. It turned out that the station was run by one of Uncle Jake's great-nephews, a third or fourth cousin about my age named Granville, and during our transactions we all recognized each other. When Jenny asked Granville what he had heard about Uncle Jake lately, he looked at her funny and said, "Why ma'am, Uncle Jake's been dead six years." He had died in Tennessee unbeknownst to anyone on our side of the family and Lula had gone back on her word to bury Jake next to Truetta. She had buried him near her own first husband and had since died herself after making arrangements to be buried between them. Aunt Jenny didn't like her role of being the senior member of the family but she didn't keep the position long. She herself died here a while back and except for my Uncle Delmer, I'm the oldest one still alive in our line.

Main Street

WALKING UP MAIN STREET in the early morning, past Neely's and Pogue's, the Rexall Store, Johnson's Hardware, Tots 'n' Teens and Preston's Dry Goods (old Mr. Preston already there at seven-thirty arranging bolts of cloth in a new display in the window, too absorbed in his work to notice Wilgus outside, nodding and smiling and waving as he goes by), Wilgus sees himself in the very panes of glass he'd seen himself in when he was three. He's fifty-three now, lumpy-looking in his winter coat and scarf and brown knit cap pulled down over his ears, unfamiliar to himself in these familiar windows, slightly shocked to see himself at all, as a matter of fact. After drinking whiskey and watching TV in his hotel room until three a.m. he'd awakened at seven, rolled out of bed, showered and shaved all in half an hour. Usually after a night of drinking Wilgus needed a couple of hours of coffee and cigarettes and radio and television before he could even think about the world outside. Now here he was on the street before any stores were open, before any winos had appeared on the sidewalk in front of the bars, before any citizens had gathered on the courthouse steps, Wilgus walking up Main Street of his old hometown one more time, headed for the bus station and breakfast and his daily talk with George.

Crossing Max's Alley he passes the place where Shelton's Barbershop used to be. June's House of Beauty is still there and so is the

59

Mountain Mission's second-hand clothing store, with its window full of 1940s-looking mannequins wearing 1970s-looking clothes. Every time Wilgus passes the Mountain Mission store he thinks about the shoot-out he witnessed in front of it when he was seven, that afternoon in 1946 when he and his Aunt Jenny had come to town to visit his Uncle Delmer, who was in jail for fighting in one of the bars. Wilgus and Jenny were standing on the courthouse steps just across the street from the Mountain Mission, not fifty feet from where two men pulled out pistols and blazed away. There were several people on the street but it happened so quickly nobody had time to hide. Two shots, then two more, then silence as one of the men fell back across the hood of a car holding his hand to his chest, the other one crumpled up limp as a rag, dead before he hit the sidewalk right there in front of the second-hand clothing store which Wilgus has walked past several times a day his entire life, almost, thinking about the dead man every time.

The store next to the Mountain Mission had been Steinman's Drug Store until a year ago but it was empty now, and so was the space where North Fork Mine Supply had had an office. But Rudy's Luncheonette where Wilgus ate chili two or three times a week was still alive and well. Rudy's had the distinction of being the smallest business establishment in the whole town of Blaine, just as every other business that had occupied the space over the years had had the same distinction. There was room for only a counter and ten stools and a grill at the far end of the room from which Rudy and various members of his large family had been serving hamburgers and hot dogs and chili and plate lunches and breakfast specials for fifteen years. Rudy's had certainly become a fixture on Main Street. No doubt to the youngest people who went there it was as if Rudy's had been there since the street itself began. But Wilgus remembered when the space where Rudy's was had been occupied by Castille's Jewelry Store, and before Castille's, Asher's Barber Shop, and before the barber shop Buckhannon's Photo Studio. His senior year in high school, Wilgus had bought a bracelet for Teresa Everidge at Castille's. He'd gone many times with his Uncle Delmer to hang out in Asher's, shooting the breeze while Ed Asher cut hair. In 1944 Wilgus's father had taken him into Buckhannon's to have his picture taken the day his father left to go overseas. Every time Wilgus went in Rudy's he thought about the previous incarnations of the place, and of himself. There were days when it seemed that every place Wilgus would go around town or out in the county would cause his mind to swarm with pictures of the old life of that place, the faces and the voices of the people who had lived there ten or twenty or thirty or forty years ago. He'd tried to explain this onion-layer aspect of his mind to his girlfriend Gretch but she couldn't get it. She called it "self-indulgent male brooding."

Inside the Post Office, Wilgus found his old high school buddy Guy Frakes at his usual post behind the counter, sorting through some papers. Wilgus and Guy had played basketball for the Champion High School Tigers thirty-five years ago.

"Hey buddy, what're you up to?" Guy asked. "Want to come to the lake this weekend?"

"Probably not," said Wilgus. "Who all's going?"

"Just me and the girls."

"What girls exactly?" Wilgus asked. He already knew where the conversation was headed. Guy's wife Della had a sister named Wavalene who lived in Cincinnati. Since her divorce a few months ago, she had spent much of her time back in Finley County. Wilgus had already been to a ball game and a picnic with Guy and Della and Wavalene. On each occasion, he had to work hard to keep from giving the impression that he was "with" Wavalene. He had hoped that news of his recent night in jail for drunk driving would have discouraged Wavalene, whose Christianity was the most visible aspect of her personality. But the opposite had happened. Now it seemed that Wavalene was drawn to Wilgus because of his sinful nature. At least that was his speculation.

In a private moment during the picnic at which Wilgus had consumed many beers, Wavalene said to him, "You know, Wilgus, you've got a lot of good in you."

"I'm feeling pretty good right now," he said.

"I'm serious. I think you are a very good person."

"I thank you for your confidence," said Wilgus.

They had gone as a foursome to watch the Tigers take their annual beating from the Finley County Panthers. It could have been worse. The Tigers had only lost by nine points this time. After the game they had driven in Guy's car out to the County Line nightclub, the traditional after-the-game gathering place for old-time Finley County basketball fans. Wilgus and Wavalene had slow-danced a couple of times to the music of the Ron Bentley Combo. They had even pressed pelvises against each other once or twice in that slow-dancing kind of way, all unacknowledged, of course, unnamed. They had danced only that one evening but he remembered how it felt to move that close together. Wilgus definitely didn't want to be that close again to Wavalene, nor open any doors or even have thoughts of possibility between them. And yet, Guy's mention of going to the lake with the girls caused several instant scenarios to flare in Wilgus's mind, sitting beside Wavalene as they drove to the lake in Guy's car, pictures of dancing with Wavalene again.

"Just us," said Guy. "I'll give you a call. You be in your office?"

"Going there now," said Wilgus.

"I'll call you," said Guy, turning his attention to the small line of customers that had formed behind Wilgus as they talked.

Headed down the Post Office steps, who should Wilgus encounter but stately, plump Mrs. Dicey Bowling, laboring up the steps with an armful of packages. Dicey had been a close friend of Wilgus's Aunt Evelyn, who had lived for many years on Oak Street there in Blaine. Evelyn and Dicey had gone to high school together back in the thirties and had stayed friends through all the decades that followed. They had lived locally as mothers and wives of Thirty-second Degree Masons and members of the Kiwanis and Rotary Clubs.

"Good morning, Mrs. Bowling," said Wilgus, in a courtly tone as he had been taught to speak to ladies and elders.

"Who is it?" the large woman said breathlessly, peering around her packages.

"It's Wilgus Collier, Mrs. Bowling. Can I help you with your packages?"

"Well, good morning to you, Wilgus, so nice to see you."

"Let me carry something for you."

"Honey I'm fine," said Dicey. "How's Evelyn getting along?"

"She's fine," said Wilgus.

"You tell Evelyn that Dicey Bowling sends her a great big hello. Will you do that?"

"I'll do it," said Wilgus.

"I've got to run now and get these things in the mail. Nice to see you, Wilgus."

Wilgus opened the door for Dicey and said goodbye. He was already feeling his age, but he knew that to Dicey he was still a mere boy. He had known her his whole life long. Dicey had a large and permanent place in his affection because she had been

63

present at every funeral for every family member he himself had been to all his life, fifty-three years, twenty-five funerals at least. He had lost count of the family funerals some years ago as they started to include cousins and in-laws. Dicey had attended every one. He would need to check with his Aunt Evelyn to be sure but there was a strand of thought in his consciousness that Dicey had almost married into the Collier family when she and the world were young. One more story he hoped there was time to get straight in his thinking before the world ended.

Half a block down Main Street Wilgus noticed the morning light as it struck the top floor of the buildings on the opposite side of the street. At eight-thirty the sun was bright in the sky but the cool air still held. Most of Main Street's buildings had gone up in the years immediately after the railroad first reached Blaine in 1913. From time to time the *Record* published photographs of the famous event, the approach of the first train, draped in bunting and flags and flying banners, band playing, festive citizens crowding around the as-yet-unpainted depot, laughing, waving, frozen moments of time.

Wilgus stood at the corner and looked at the space where the people had gathered in celebration, holding in mind the images from the photographs even as he studied the buildings on the other side. Then he saw his father in 1943 standing in a crowd of people at Courthouse Corner with his son Wilgus perched on his shoulder, the time he hoisted Wilgus to his shoulders so he could see over the heads of the crowd and watch the patriotic parade work its way down Main Street, thousands of people crowding the sidewalks, cheering the high school bands, the horse-drawn wagons carrying soldiers and sailors, groups of Boy Scouts, cheerleaders in open cars, American Legion, VFW, the Lion's Club, the Rotary Club,

Kiwanis, cardboard tanks and ships on wagons, veterans of wars, Army, Navy, Marine Corps recruiters carrying the flag of the United States of America. We stood right here, Wilgus thought, precisely this corner, this space. Wilgus was four in 1943. By '44, at the mighty age of five, he had risen through the ranks to command his own battleship in the parade. He looked down from his eminence at the crowd below, dressed in the little sailor suit his aunts had bought for him from a mail-order catalog,

On the sidewalk in front of the courthouse Wilgus paused to gaze at the two-story brick building across the street where in the old days doctors' and lawyers' offices had lined the halls of the second floor above Preston's Dry Goods store. He had interviewed Judge Stone there one day, a local person who had been witness to the old life of the town. The judge was cleaning out his second-floor office space because it was late in his life and time to order all that was disordered. He seemed pleased that Wilgus wanted to talk to him, he seemed lonesome and glad to take time on an afternoon to tell Wilgus stories from the early days of the town before the built-part had overwhelmed the pristine original, when there still were edible fish in the river and game in the woods and the twentieth century itself was still young.

Wilgus listened as the old judge looked out his window and told about the days when Main Street was nothing but mud, "deep enough to lose a horse in," as he put it. The first sidewalks made out of planks, no sewer system, Blaine barely a village in a bend of a mountain river.

"But by the late forties," Judge Stone said, "these offices up here were as modern as any big city's. Blaine had quite a cosmopolitan air in those days. It's just storage rooms now, but there was a time, this whole floor was lawyers and dentists."

"Wasn't Doctor Fulton's dental office up here?" Wilgus asked, knowing the answer full well.

"Yes, Pete Fulton. His office was next door, through that wall right there. You know why they called him 'Pistol,' don't you?" the judge asked.

"No," said Wilgus.

"Pete Fulton was a drunk and a womanizer," said the judge. "That's why they called him Pistol."

"I spent a year in Dr. Fulton's chair one day," Wilgus said.

"Many people did," the old judge replied. The judge talked about the forties, fifties, and sixties when coal was still king and passenger trains and five buses a day brought people, freight, and the U.S. mail in from the world to Blaine. In those days, Kentucky mountain towns were still local places. Highway 15 was still a two-lane road and no four-lanes bypassed the old downtowns.

Many towns were dead zones now but there was still life on Main Street in Blaine. Early that morning there had been a layer of fog above the river which curved around the town. Between the buildings Wilgus could see a string of empty coal gons on the other side of the river headed south deeper into the mountains. He heard the screech of the wheels and the clanging of the gons as the train picked up speed. The town had begun another business day. In his years as a newspaperman in Blaine, Wilgus had witnessed the beginnings of ten thousand business days on Main Street. Office workers from the lawyers' offices, the courthouse, the insurance companies, clerks in the clothing and hardware stores taking their stations at their desks, the retail store managers opening their doors, the booths and tables in Blaine Drug filling with the second wave of coffee drinkers. Breakfast eaters salted their eggs in Abner's Grill and spooned gravy onto their biscuits made by Abner himself. Soon

Mr. Evans would open the great door of the vault in the Cumberland Bank where everybody's money was.

That night after watching the local news on TV, Wilgus put on his sweater and scarf and hat and gloves and went back out on Main Street to take his third walk around town that day. After the particular kind of day he had had, his mind was active this evening in a way that it hadn't been in a week or two and he wanted to stay with his thoughts. He felt alert, eager for a good walk around his old home town, eager for the exercise and for the kinds of memory associations that he knew awaited him as once again he walked the familiar streets and sidewalks he had known for half a century. For Wilgus and most of his family and neighbors on Trace Fork in the years he was growing up, the town of Blaine was the center of the universe. If you lived most of your life out in the county, in the hollers or mining camps or roadside villages like Krypton, town was a place you sort of dreaded to go and yet it was exciting too. Over the years Wilgus had come to feel comfortable in town, like a member of the place. His favorite walks were at night when, except for a few passing cars, he had the streets to himself.

At eight p.m. Wilgus stood on the bridge that connected Main Street to the train depot across the river, his folded arms resting on the railing, looking down at the waters of the North Fork river flowing now as they had for a thousand or ten thousand years. It was the second time that day he had stood on that very spot, arms folded, looking down at the water flowing past Blaine. And he would do it again before the night was over.

Dentist Story

IT WAS 1950 or thereabouts. I was eleven years old. I showed up in Dr. Fulton's office one Saturday morning to get two teeth filled. He sat me in one of his chairs, gave me a shot, patted me on the head and told me to sit right there, he'd be right back. He went to see his other patient on the other side of the partition. I couldn't see the other patient, didn't know who he was or what they were saying. But something Dr. Fulton said made the man laugh and Dr. Fulton laughed and I felt my mouth getting numb, which was a relief.

In front of me were two tall windows that looked out over Main Street. I had a full view of the courthouse and up and down the street almost from one end to the other. I saw up to the Post Office and bus station and down the street as far as the Kentucky Theater and the PassTime Club and Hayes Shoe Store. The sidewalks were so crowded people had to get out in the street to have room to walk. But even then the traffic was bumper to bumper so they still had trouble getting through. It was Saturday and the whole county was in town that day. People stood in clutches all over the courthouse steps, talking to one another, visiting, trading, swapping knives, listening to the preachers preach. Somebody had a loudspeaker going, advertising a music show at the high school gym that night. I thought I'd like to go if I felt like it after getting my teeth filled.

Tooth-filling was something to dread back then and I needed a lot of it. As far as I was concerned, Dr. Fulton could take all the time he wanted getting back to me. After an hour, I didn't care if he never came back. It was a very trance-like hour, visionary. I could see into the very nature of time. I felt like I had been a witness over Main Street since primordial times, when lizards big as horses crawled on the Kentucky river bank and big mastodons and mammoths walked the land, and the old Indians camped in the very river bend where Blaine now stood, and Daniel Boone walked right where Main Street was on his way to Pound Gap. Then the time my father carried me up that very street from the theater past that very courthouse to the bus station to get my picture made the day he left for war. From my perch on his shoulder I surveyed the Main Street panorama knowing I'd never forget it.

And I'd never forget this day, either, sitting in Dr. Fulton's dental chair. I'll be right back he said and my mouth got numb and time went by and through the window I looked out upon the throngs of people coming and going on Main Street until gradually the light changed in the sky and time went by and the street crowds thinned and there I sat, late in the afternoon, my novocaine worn off by now. Dr. Fulton had said wait and so I waited, and there I was at four p.m. still waiting. I knew it was unusual, I knew it was an odd adventure that I would remember always, I knew it was a rare and memorable day. I knew I had been given the perfect seat to observe the life of Main Street on Saturday afternoon in my hometown. Finally, about four p.m., Dr. Fulton's wife Marie who taught Sunday school showed up wearing very dressy clothes. I remember the sound of her keys in the door. I remember her alluring smell.

She said, "Why Wilgus, what are you doing here?"

"Getting my teeth filled," I said. "Dr. Fulton told me to wait."

"You've been here all day?" she asked.

I said, "Yes, he said he would be right back."

She said, "Oh my God," and took me in her arms and hugged me tight against her bosom. Dr. Fulton had forgotten about me and, as I later understood, gone to the Royal Bar to begin his weekend drinking. I did not complain. Mrs. Fulton's embrace had been worth waiting for.

Lester Dunham

Dear WILGUS COLLIER,

Are you that Wilgus Collier that writes articles and puts them in the paper and that's your little picture out there next to your name? If you are him I want to know how much you would charge me to write my life up and put it in a book.

I have had such a life as would make a good book that I want to get out to the people. I have been trying to write my life in dribs and drabs for some time now but it just scatters all over the place and I don't seem to be any good at putting the pieces together. I want to tell all the ups and downs of my life. And I want to put my thinking in this book, too, and testify to my beliefs. I love God and I love Jesus and I love the memory of my wife and my mother and my father, too, although Daddy wasn't nearly as good to me as Mommy was.

I've had troubles in my life, and I've had blessings I ain't deserved. But I thank the Lord for all that's come to me. My health ain't the best but I get around well enough. My children's all healthy. I ain't got no debts to speak of. My hearing's about gone but I don't dwell on it. My eyesight's still yet strong. I've got a good warm house to live in here at my daughter Blanche's. I made a big garden this year. We've got a freezer full of food plus a cellar full of stuff me and Blanche put up last year.

You better believe I've got a lot to go in this book. There's a lot I'd like to leave out but I will fight myself hard to tell the truth, for I am sure you are not the kind of feller that wants to deal in lies. Daughter Blanche says she went to school with you. She clips your articles out of the paper and keeps them in a scrapbook. She had them out looking at them the other day, that's what put me in mind to write to you about my book. Write to me soon with your answer to my proposition, Mr. Collier. Time passes and who knows when any of us'll be called.

Very truly yours,
Lester Dunham

Dear Mr. Collier,

I'm sorry you didn't write me back but maybe it's just as well. I've been too weak to lift my head for over a week now. It come on me by surprise. I'd been feeling good for some time. They took pictures of me but they still don't know what it is. I'll get along good two or three weeks, then I'll get so I can't hardly draw a breath.

I seen your article in the paper about the men riding the log rafts out of the hills in the old days. It put me in mind of things my daddy told me when I was a boy. It made me know for sure that you're the very one to help me get my book wrote so I hope you write me soon or call or come on out to Bonnet Creek and see me. We ought not delay too long. This war news has got me nervous. There's many signs we are in the last days.

I've been having so many thoughts here lately I can't hardly keep it all straight in my mind. It's a workout, trying to keep up with all this I'm thinking. I try to write it down but all I write is bare bones. Blanche fusses at me for scattering papers all over the house. She says I've got to quit my messing and gomming if I'm going to live with her.

There's many parts of my life I ain't remembered yet. But there's many that I have, the main ones being

    1. Working with my daddy in 30 inch coal when I was 14 yrs old.

    2. Joining the CCC in 1938 and working in the logwoods in Oregon til 1939.

    3. Working for wages in a copper mine in Butte, Montana six months in 1939.

    4. Coming home in 1940 to teach school when Bonnet Creek was out of a teacher.

    5. Joining the Army and fighting in New Guinea in 1943, getting a splinter in my head that same year.

6. Going in the nightclub business after the war here at home and making a lot of money and then losing it all when I got in trouble with the law 1948-1950.

7. Meeting and marrying Dorsie Brumley and joining the church and running for the school board in 1950.

8. Then spending the rest of my life operating a taxi company between here and Hazard til Dorsie died and I had a stroke, both three years ago.

Write to me quick, Mr. Collier. If it's money you're worried about, you ne'en to for me and you are going to come out in the black on this book. I know of many people already that wants to buy it. I'll keep setting down my recollections til I hear from you, then we'll work together to get it right.

Very truly yours,
Lester Dunham

Dear Mr. Collier,

Well, I don't know whether to give up on you or not. I was in hopes me and you might come to a quick agreement but now I feel these troubles setting in, especially since you won't write me back and let me know the drift of your thinking so far. Yesterday old Buford Whitaker was by here and I told him me and you was trying to work out a deal on my book. He said he had you in high school, said I'd be doing good to work with you unless you've turned out a drunk. He said you was the smartest one to ever come through Champion High School but that he has heard that you have let liquor get the best of you. He said you walk down Main Street looking up at the tops of the buildings, that you just stare off into space and don't see people to talk to them anymore. I don't know where Buford heard it or if it's true or not. I'd be sorry, not just because you might be unreliable to work with but because of what I have heard about you as I talk to people about cooking up a deal with you.

Everybody I've talked to except Buford says you are a good feller. They say you are one of the Trace Fork Colliers, that Herschel Collier was your grandfather and that Glen was your father. I've always thought of your whole set as a good family of people. I used to haul all you all in my taxi. I knew Glen very well. He rode my taxi many times in the old days. I used to drive your folks to Lexington to see Glen when he was in the VA hospital. I was in there with him for awhile, and your Uncle Delmer too. Is Delmer dead yet? I could tell you stories on that rascal. And he had a younger brother, and there were several sisters. I knowed your Granddaddy Collier tolerably well. Me and him used to play checkers together at the old ice house in town of a Saturday. And we used to do a little trading at the stock sale. I sold him a pony one time, you

77

might remember it, he was rusty red with a white blaze on his face. It was a feisty thing but he liked it, said he was going to work it in the pony mines. My mother had a sister that was married to a Leslie County Collier, so that might make me and you a little kin. Everybody speaks well of your people. I'd hate to think that you have turned out no account. From all I can learn you're somebody that really knows his ABC's about the printing business. But if you don't think you can stay sober til the work is done, maybe we ought to think twice about this whole proposition. So I will say no more til I hear from you.

Yours truly,
L. Dunham

Dear Mr. Dunham,

Please forgive me for not answering your most interesting letters. The secretary at the newspaper office sends them on to me up here in Lexington. I'm taking a kind of rest cure here at Bluegrass Clinic. I'll be here another month or so.

You certainly don't need to introduce yourself to me, Mr. Dunham. You have been important to my family all of my life. You were our main means of transport before any of us had a car. When I get home I'll come out to your house sometime and we can talk about the old days awhile, maybe tape record ourselves. Would that interest you? Please do continue to write to me. I enjoy your letters very much, they make me feel close to home as I go through the various treatments here. I'll wait until I get home before discussing your book idea, but let me say now that your story is most interesting. Maybe we could run some excerpts from it in the *Record* as a serial. Please tell Blanche hello for me. She was a freshman when I was a senior, but we were indeed good friends in school.

Yours truly,
Wilgus Collier

Dear Mr. Collier,

Hearing from you was the best thing to happen to me all week. Boy we're in business now. I had faith you'd write me, and now you have and it's a tonic. Blanche is tickled too. She thinks you hung the moon. She said to tell you she's sorry you have to go to a clinic. What's wrong with you? I hope it ain't serious. I'll keep pecking away at this book and when you get back, me and you will go to town on it and get it printed and go on television to tell everybody to run out and buy a copy.

What I want to get in the first chapter or two Mr. Collier is about how my mommy always took up for me when nobody else would. All my life, she was good to me way past what I deserved. When I was such a hell raiser there after the war, she prayed for me and never did give up on me. When I got in trouble with the law that time, my mommy stood right by me. She always did from the time I was little. Did you know I cried all the time when I was little? I was a very nervous child. I wet the bed til I was twelve year old. I want that put right in there.

When I was eight I went through a spell of seeing visions. I want that put in too. Pictures would come up behind my eyes. I'd see people burning up in fires. I'd see big holes open up in the sky. My daddy thought I was crazy. He said I ought to be sent off. He tried to whip me one time for what I was seeing but Mommy took a poker to him and run him out of the house. One time in later years she picked up a rock on a deputy sheriff that was whipping my head with a blackjack. She didn't throw it but that deputy knowed she would if he didn't quit and he quit. That's just how she was. Mommy was a sweet Christian woman but there was a limit to what she would take off of anybody. Daddy run hot and cold on his Christianity but Mommy was always the steadiest good church woman there ever was. If it wasn't for her I'd of been dead and in hell a long time ago.

So don't you worry about nothing, especially anything Buford Whitaker has to say. Buford is a good man but he's been known to stretch the truth. He's been known to outright make the truth up when it suits his purpose. That's the same as a lie in my book so I decided to not worry my mind about you, except about this clinic business. I understand what it is to be sick. I can tell by your handwrite that you are a dependable man.

I'll send you regular reports til I hear from you again. Take care of yourself. I can't afford to lose my publisher now that I've found him.

Very truly yours,
Lester Dunham

Dear Mr. Collier,

Well sir, I'm up against a problem the like of which I had no idea I'd run into when I undertook to make this book. I'm sure glad I have you to call on for advice. The thing I need to know before I can go on is whether such stuff as my son-in-law Grover Blankenship proving out to be no count goes in this book or not. I don't see why I ought to play up anybody like that yet I feel a need to tell the whole truth, too, even if I do have to live in the same house with Grover.

Grover looked like he was going to be all right at first. He worked 3 straight years driving the laundry truck for Blaine Laundry. Then he worked a year and 3 months for Denver Bentley sacking kennel coal for $5 an hour. Then one day he just disappeared on us. Nobody knowed where he was at for 3 days. Come to find out he'd been laying out at this woman Onella's trailer house there above the Dipsey Doodle curve. Onella has turned her house into a ginny barn, so they ain't no telling what all went on there. Some says she bootlegs beer on Sunday.

I wanted to call the law on Grover but Blanche wouldn't let me. She said she was afraid he was dead in a ditch somewhere is the only reason she got upset that Grover was gone in the first place. That may sound funny to you, Mr. Collier, but just between me and you, Blanche and Grover had been on the outs a long time. I knew all along that she wouldn't put up with him forever. At first she loved him to pieces but then she seen how sorry he was.

All that was many years ago. So where I'm buffaloed, Mr. Collier, is knowing what to put in or leave out of my book, there's so much a body could say. What bothers me worser'n anything is that I passed judgment on Grover. I condemned him and hardened my heart toward him, and as bad as he was, it wasn't right for me to low-rate him like that. That's God's job, not mine. I know in my own heart that I have done things a heap worser'n what Grover did when I was his age, so where does that leave me?

It's like pulling teeth to talk about this but I want it all to come out. I want the light to shine in ever place that's dark. I tell you one thing I'm going to put in for sure: that where I know I went wrong was in not having to work when I got out of the Army but going ahead anyway, and taking up the wrong thing. I never should of went in the nightclub business. Mommy tried to tell me it was wrong but I was too full of pride to listen to her.

You see, Mr. Collier, after the war I drawed a 85% disability pension for my splinter that I got in New Guinea. I still yet draw it. I live good on it if I live humble, which at my present age I most often do. I could have lived good on that pension back then if I'd had any sense. But my brother-in-law Henley that married my sister Dedra talked me into going in the nightclub business with him in 1946, and right there is where I went wronger than Grover could ever hope to.

I'd run with Henley and his bunch some before the war. Your Uncle Delmer could tell you tales from those days if he wanted to, for he run with that bunch himself off and on. I hesitate to tell you that information because above all I do not want to get any family wires crossed and cause you and him or any of your people to be on the outs with one another or any such thing, and also I don't want to get into stuff that would interfere with our professional doings together on my book. You see how complicated things can get.

But the truth is the truth which is what we are trying to deal in, so I have to report to you that Delmer did run some with me and Henley before the war, and a little bit afterwards as a matter of fact. Him and his various ones used to come to the County Line on weekends to drink their drinks and dance their dances and now and then fight their fights as well. I'll say no more. Ask Delmer if you want to know more, it is for him to tell, not me now that I have done my duty to my editor and publisher by these disclosures.

What I am trying to get to here Mr. Collier is when Henley come to me there in 1946 and asked me to go in business with him and I said I would, right there was the very forks in the road that I chose wrong at. We opened us a nightclub we called The County Line over there on the highway where Finley County and Perry County runs together. Maybe you've been there yourself. We run that place from 1946 to 1949. We done good business all through that time.

This whole country in through here was run over with old World War II boys like myself and Delmer. Your daddy Glen was different from the rest of us. We weren't all gentlemen like Glen. He might take a beer now and then as I recollect, but you didn't catch him running wild in public. But most of them old boys just home from the war was rougher'n cobs, it took some of them years to settle down. And they had money to spend too. Me and Henley made so much money, I got so I felt broke if I didn't have a thousand dollars in my pocket. And if I wasn't packing a pistol, I felt plum naked. We drunk liquor like it was water and we was bad to foller after the women.

Well, time went along, and it got to be 1949. That was a big strike time here in the coalfields. One night at the Line these union boys run up against a bunch of scabs and there was the biggest shootout that ever was. One man from Perry County got killed and there was several others shot up pretty bad. The worst part for me was instead of trying to stop it by calling the law or something, I pulled out my .38 and shot too. I was only shooting into the ceiling but still, a shot is a shot. It was the Devil in me. I knowed it was the Devil at the time, I could see him behind my eyes, in there laughing at me.

Well, they shut us down after that and me and Henley both got indicted for accessory to a killing, and there was a big trial and it took ever cent we both had to come clear in court. I come clear before the law, but I knowed I was guilty in the eyes of God. I knowed if I hadn't of ever opened up that nightclub, and if I'd of let liquor alone, then them people wouldn't of been killed and hurt. And I had shot my gun, to boot. I was part of the generalized uproar.

It about killed me to think about what I had done. I laid drunk for weeks, trying to get over how I felt. Being wounded in the war wasn't half as bad as I felt in that time. I was drinking liquor and taking all the paregoric I could get. I had a buddy that would slip over from Middlesboro and bring me shots of morphine when he could. I was drinking a case of beer and a pint of liquor a day. That's the kind of life I was living. And there's more along this thoughtline to tell too.

But to make a long story short, I was on the edge of becoming a drunk and a full-time dope when I met my future wife Dorsie at a pie supper over at Whitaker Crossroads one night. She turned my whole life around. In May of 1951 I got baptized at the mouth of Bonnet Creek there behind the Freewill Church, just down below where I was born. And I joined the church. And me and Dorsie got married and my life was blessed from that day to the day she died.

And after that, here I am bearing a judgment against my own son-in-law. There's a lot I don't feel right about, and to get right is what I'm trying to do. I've had blessings I ain't deserved. I know I'm in debt to God. I just hope I can settle up before the whirlwind comes, which to judge by the news could be any time now. I figure me and you see eye to eye on a lot of things, Mr. Collier. It's a pleasure to do business with you.

Very truly yours,
Lester Dunham

Dear Wilgus,

My father wanted me to write and tell you that he has been sick lately. I have been wanting to thank you so much for being nice to him. I worry that his letters might be a nuisance to you. You are very nice to let him correspond with you. Your letter meant much to him. He has various things wrong with him. Mainly he's just getting old. That's true for all of us, I guess. I feel like the same person I was when we were in school together. But I know the years are starting to add up.

If my father pesters you too much, please tell me. I expect that you have noticed that he gets some of his facts wrong sometimes, especially regarding me. Me and Grover divorced a long time ago. He died eight years ago in Hammond, Indiana. To hear Daddy tell it, that all happened a month or two ago.

It's hard to believe it's been seven years since we ran into each other that night at Barbara's house. I don't think I've seen you since then. It's strange that we could live in the same county and be such strangers. I took a practical nursing course at the community college and have worked at the hospital off and on ever since. My training comes in very handy dealing with my dad's various problems. It gets hard sometimes, having him live here, but since my kids are grown and gone, he is pretty good company. He sure talks a lot. (Ha)

Come out and see me and Daddy sometime, we'd both like to see you.

Blanche Dunham

Dear Blanche,

It was great to hear from you. Thanks for writing. My month here at this "resort" has been a good experience. I feel rested for the first time in years. I'll tell you about it sometime. It certainly is strange that we could live in our small county and not see each other, especially since we used to be such good friends. Hearing your voice in your letter makes it seem that it has been only a few days. You may not believe it, Blanche, but I have thought about you over the years. I do remember that confused night at Lee's and Barbara's house. I didn't behave very well and I'm sorry. I have come to see how foolish and manic and sort of nervous and not in control of myself I have been so much of my life. It has been quite an experience this last month, talking about such things. I think it appeared to people that I was merely energetic and enthusiastic about things, but looking back, I really think I was a little crazy. I may be getting over some of my excessive ways.

Meanwhile, you have grown up and raised kids and held your family together and worked in a real way to help people. I admire you and appreciate it that you still felt like writing to me. The timing could not be better. It seems sort of magic that your dad started writing to me when he did. I love hearing from him, it puts me in touch with fundamental things that I need to be closer to, family stories, the old days in general. Please don't fret that your dad is any kind of bother to me, for he is not. When I get home I'd like to take you up on your invitation to come out to Bonnet Creek and see you all. I'm not sure I know how to help your dad put out a book, but I do want to interview him and also visit with you.

Wilgus

Bluegrass Clinic

WHEN MY SHRINK HELEN asked for some particulars that might help her understand my condition, I began by telling her about the dog and the police and jail. I said I thought when the police pulled me over that night it was because I'd stopped by the side of the road earlier in the day to knock a half-dead puppy in the head with a jack handle. I'd seen the little thing several days before, stumbling around in the weeds at a certain spot in the road where people threw garbage over the hill. When I didn't see it the next day I figured somebody had picked it up and given it a home. When I saw it a week later still thrashing around in the weeds beside the road, so weak it could barely stand, it made me furious. I put the thing out of its misery and then went on to Lee's and Barbara's house to hang out and try to calm my nerves. Barbara had gone somewhere that night so Lee and I drank a little whiskey and sipped a little beer while Lee picked out a few tunes on his guitar. On my way back to town around midnight two young Kentucky state troopers, neither of them over twenty-five, pulled me over not far from where I'd killed the dog and gave me their humiliating little sobriety test which, of course, I failed. I thanked them later, in the courthouse, the day of my trial, for getting me off the highway but at the jail that night I didn't say a word to anybody. I just followed the procedures as directed and soon enough found myself in a cell presided over by this big old boy named Rufe who was pulling a year for breaking into a mine supply depot to steal dynamite to blow up the house of another old boy who had in some way offended Rufe's honor. I remembered writing a news story for the *Record* about the break-in some months before but I didn't tell Rufe that. He was doing too good a job supervising our cell block for me to interfere with him in any way.

Helen listened to my story with proper professional attention, unlike my girlfriend Gretchen who, when I told her about my recent dog and jail adventures, was so horrified she said she was now certain that she would never marry me. But she was willing to fly down from Chicago for a weekend in Louisville to "work on our relationship" as she put it. I dreaded the meeting so badly that on my way to meet her at the Louisville airport I stopped off in Lexington to have a beer at Two Keys Tavern and take a sentimental walk around the university campus where I had gone to school in the good old days. I realized as I walked that I could not face Gretchen that night or ever again. So I bought a pint of bourbon and checked into a Holiday Inn at the edge of town to drink and watch TV all weekend, consciously choosing to not call Gretchen at the airport to tell her I would not be there.

Later, by way of apology and intending to comfort Gretchen, I told her that she had larger powers than she realized. She said she knew that. I said you've never been able to say yes to yourself. I'm saying it now, she said. You have to break old habits if you're going to make any progress, I said. She said speak for yourself. At the same time, I told her, she had a little too much confidence in the certainty of her views for my comfort. That's one reason I cultivate a certain space around me, to protect myself from your models. I don't want to live by conscious models or plans, I told

Gretchen. I just want to float along and see where life and experience carry me.

Suit yourself, Gretchen said, and slammed down the phone. In a letter a few days later, Gretchen said Wilgus, I have finally realized and accepted that throughout our involvement, I have never had true access to your feelings, your secret inner life. You are the most closed person I ever met. I can hardly believe it took me this long to finally figure out something that was right there in front of my face the whole time. You have related to me the whole time we've known each other as if I am a two-dimensional person that you have taken for granted. You have never really recognized me as a unique person. You have had no real interest in or curiosity about me. What worries me most about that is not what it says about you, but about me. Yet I am worried about you too. I was angry on the phone the other day but I'm not angry now, I'm something else. We both are messes but I'm about to unmess myself. I'm glad you didn't come to the airport, it freed me to finally see the situation for what it had become. I don't want to see you for at least ten years. Then maybe we'll run into each other somewhere with some chance of being friends. Please get yourself healthy, Wilgus. Please quit drinking. Go on a diet. Get some therapy. It would help your life hugely if you got the hell out of eastern Kentucky for awhile. If you're a Vista Volunteer and it's time to fight poverty and in general save the world, fine. I tried that years ago and in the process met this totally impressive young newspaperman that I thought I knew but over time actually became quite horrified by. For a while I was sorry I had ever met you. But I'm over it now. I'm going off into my life now, Wilgus. Goodbye.

91

My Early Therapy

IN THE NAÏVE DAYS of my early therapy I thought my condition was a simple split along your basic sacred and profane lines, complicated by drinking. But after a few sessions Helen said it was clear to her that I was in many more pieces than two, and that I should immediately enroll as a resident at Bluegrass Clinic, near Lexington. I liked Helen enormously, I was ready to tell her everything I'd ever thought or felt or done. But I resisted becoming a resident in a clinic. I asked her if being in a clinic amounted to handing myself over to people-fixers the way a piece of furniture is handed over to the reupholsterers. If so, I told her, I would say screw the whole therapy deal and go sit on my aunt's front porch the next twenty or thirty years. Helen laughed. She said, you have to have some trust if you're going to make any progress in the psychology business, Wilgus. She told me she and a colleague were founders of Bluegrass Clinic and that in addition to her work with individuals she was in charge of the Psychodrama and Sandplay sessions there. When I asked Helen if she remembered my litany of childhood traumas, she told me to refresh her memory. I gave her a quick summary but it all sounded so hilarious in the retelling we both cracked up before I got halfway through it. War. Funerals. Loss. Grief. Tragedy. I felt completely healed after that one session but Helen said beware of all forms of elation. So I drove to Lexington to talk with Helen once a week until finally she said you better come live at the Clinic a while, Wilgus, we've got to get you over the hump. You need heavy artillery fast.

I think I'm in love with you, I said.

That's natural, she said.

But it feels strange, I said.

It happens, she said.

But don't you love me too? I asked.

Of course, she said, but that doesn't mean we're going to sleep together. There are three primary rules in therapy. I'm the boss, people must pay their bills, and no sex.

Not with anybody? I asked.

Nobody, no time, Helen answered. Not until you graduate.

Can't we even hug a little? I asked.

Of course, she laughed, and Helen wrapped her strong arms around me in a warm embrace.

Psychodrama

I T WAS DARK by the time the new group of clients gathered for
their first session in the Psychodrama Room on the ground floor
of the Manse, as the old mansion on Russell Cave Pike that housed
Bluegrass Clinic was called. The new members sat shy and silent on
cushions in a semi-circle in front of Helen, who stood before them
on a slightly raised platform in front of a stone fireplace that filled
most of the end of the room, her eyes closed and her hands held
before her face as if in prayer. Each individual had been in private
therapy with Helen for at least a year, so all were familiar with her
voice and some of her ways. None of them knew much about Helen
but they all knew that she knew a great deal about each one of them.

In the early days of their private therapy together, before Wilgus
checked into the clinic, Helen told him that he thought too much,
that he needed to get out of his head, return to the world. "You act
like you don't have a body, Wilgus. As if life is something to think
rather than live. I get the feeling that you've been gone longer than
you think. It's time to come home and one way to do that is to be
among people more. You've turned into a damned hermit; lots of
folks think you're dead."

"I feel dead," said Wilgus, "buried in a hole in the ground."

"Well, get out of it and go see some people, be social. You used
to be very gregarious."

And so in the days before he checked into the clinic Wilgus started calling on people around Blaine, showing up at their houses unannounced. He had lost his driver's license after a night in jail for drunk driving. With no driver's license he walked wherever he went around town but to go out across the county to Big Willard and Second Creek and the mouth of Leatherwood and Defiance and Baxter and Bull Creek he had to hire taxis, telling them to wait while he went into this or that house to say hello to his friends and relatives.

Wilgus's partner in Psychodrama was a tall woman in her forties somewhere, with brown eyes and short brown hair flecked with gray. She wore dancer's tights and a flowered cotton pullover shirt that hung loosely from her shoulders.

"Do you want to be first?" she asked Wilgus.

"Not really," said Wilgus nervously.

They looked at each other blankly, then broke into embarrassed laughter. "It feels strange, not saying our names, doesn't it?" said the woman.

"Pretty strange," said Wilgus. "I kind of like it though."

"Kind of liberating," said the woman. "So you want me to go first?"

"If you want to."

"Okay," said the woman. "I'm willing." She pushed two large pillows against the wall and leaned back. "Well, let's see. I'm from Cincinnati. I went to Ohio State. I'm a social worker. I work with kids mostly. I'm pretty thoroughly middle-class."

Suddenly the woman seemed nervous. As she cleared her throat, Wilgus asked her to tell about her parents.

"Our family was pretty ordinary, I'd have to say. My dad worked for Procter & Gamble. My mother was a teacher. They get along okay. At least they've stayed married. Very traditional. They didn't like it when I majored in psychology. They wanted me to be a lawyer. Actually, what I really wanted to major in was theater, but that would have been too much for them."

"You wanted to be an actor?" asked Wilgus.

"Oh yes. At least I thought I did. I don't really have a talent for it. I just like the way it smells backstage, the feel of live theater, something about it. But that was a long time ago."

"How did you meet Helen?" Wilgus asked.

"I went to one of her workshops in Columbus. How did you meet her?"

Wilgus grunted out a little laugh. "Actually, I picked her out of the yellow pages."

"How interesting. Which phone book? Where are you from?"

"Here in Kentucky. Up in the coalfields, in the mountains, little place called Blaine."

The woman laughed. "So are you a hillbilly?"

"Absolutely," said Wilgus.

"And what do you do in your mountain town?"

"I publish a weekly newspaper, the *Finley County Record*. I'm sure you've heard all about it."

"Not really," she said, laughing again. "I'm sure it's interesting."

"Oh, it is that," said Wilgus.

"And you just plucked Helen out of the yellow pages?"

Wilgus nodded. "The Lexington yellow pages. I saw her for about a year and then stopped. Then a few months ago I started seeing her again. But I haven't been to any of her workshops. Until now."

The woman thought for a moment before she spoke again. "I actually wasn't ready for Helen when I first met her. It was all way over my head. But I feel ready now."

"That's good," Wilgus said. "I wish I felt that way."

"Are you scared?"

"Not really scared. Let's just say the suspense is pretty intense."

The woman leaned forward and playfully nudged Wilgus's shoulder with her own. "I know the feeling," she said. "I'm in pretty big suspense myself. This clinic'll probably destroy me. But that's okay. I need to be destroyed."

The woman looked into Wilgus's eyes and he looked back. He knew he had just received a message, but he had no idea what it was or even who it was from. He was struggling to think of something to say when Helen's voice rang out, "Time! Thank you. I hope you enjoyed your chat. Now, if you like, you may reveal your name to your partner, but first names only, please."

"I'm Dorothy," said the woman. Wilgus said he was Wilgus. They were standing now, facing each other, both grinning broadly, their faces flushed, radiant. Then their bodies joined in a friendly hug. When they stood apart again, both had tears in their eyes.

Helen

THERE WERE TWELVE people in our group at Bluegrass Clinic, not counting Helen of course, or her colleague Marguerette, or Doshia who owned the Manse. We were aware of other people coming and going in the background at the clinic, but we quickly learned that it was Helen who was boss of all that happened as far as we plebeian sufferers were concerned. One morning during the first week Helen abruptly clapped her hands and called out, "Okay everybody, up against the wall. I want all the grownups on the left and the whiners, mama's boys, and daddy's girls on the right."

Without a word all twelve of us went to the wall and took our places. I fell in the middle of the pack somewhere, technically among the grownups but at the lower end of the spectrum, too close to the whiners for comfort. It was disturbing when Helen trooped our line smirking and laughing as if we all had gone directly to the exact place we belonged, which of course we had. I flattered myself that Helen saw me as one of the more solid and reliable of her brood. I wanted her to say, Wilgus, you don't belong in the middle, come to the head of the line. But Helen smirked and laughed her loudest while looking right at me, riveting me in the humiliating position I had chosen for myself.

It shocked me and filled me with anxiety to discover darker aspects of Helen's personality that I had not known before. Helen as an authoritarian boss was terrifying. In an instant her face could become a mask hiding an unknowable person who held the power of life and death over everyone in her vicinity. She was a mystery. We never knew when she was going to spring one of her spontaneous therapeutic exercises on us. Every now and then she would fool us by going all casual for a minute as if she was our friend and peer, and saying something comforting like, this work isn't easy, is it? Or, we're trying to recover something natural that people have lost. Then, boom, on your feet! On the floor! All narcissists raise your hands! Manic depressives, two steps forward and one step back! Behind her back some in our group referred to Helen as the DI, drill instructor. We feared and respected her. She made it clear that she was serious about her idea that we all had lost something basic that we must recover.

By the end of the first week, we all began to recover, in vivid detail, memories of our early individual and family life experiences. Helen's rule was that when you recovered a memory, you had to testify immediately to the person nearest you, blurt out a spontaneous story, which might be of an intimate, personal nature. Sometimes it might be told to a person you were walking with across the meadow to the gazebo. Other times it might be to two or three companions during lunch on the patio. In this way, Dorothy told her tales of alcoholism and attempted suicides. Jay confessed his left-wing sins from his radical days in the 1960s; he was a conservative now. Keith described his downward path to drug addiction which destroyed his career as a banker in Lexington. Gordon from Hazard was chronically depressed. Anita had been abused as a child. Arnold was a manic-depressive who had grown up in a series of oppressive foster homes. Merrilee had shot her husband in the leg with a .22 rifle, trying seriously to kill him, and was in residence at the clinic as a condition of her probated prison sentence. Rene was suicidal and so was Theodore who doubted his Christianity. Charlotte was hooked on tranquilizers. Young Beth Ann cried most of the time.

I was an alcoholic weekly newspaper editor from eastern Kentucky who, when it came my time to testify in a Psychodrama session, began by referring to the Turner Thesis but veered into what I thought was an impressive treatise on Daniel Boone. Boone was a good man, I said, a fine man, a competent man, a compassionate man, a whole man well along on his process of individuation, a worthy model for contemporary American males. When I said that, Jay the ex-Progressive hooted and laughed and howled and jeered in such manic glee he nearly fell over in his chair.

BOONE WAS AN INDIAN KILLER, ASSHOLE! Jay hissed at me and seven of the eleven people in the Psychodrama circle nodded in agreement. The lovely Dorothy looked at me with soulful sympathetic eyes even as she nodded her agreement with Jay. Bitch! I thought, but equally I thought: I understand. I love you. I'll see you in the evening, I said to her with my eyes. We'll take a walk across the grounds to the spring and the old gazebo, I'll hold your hand and listen as you talk about your drinking days and your attempted suicides, and I'll talk about my World War II obsession, the Third Reich, the Rising Sun, the Eastern Front, Americans training at home with wooden guns during the Battle of Stalingrad. I'll tell you what I see at night when I walk the grounds alone. Dorothy smiled and accepted my invitation, even as she nodded in agreement with the ex-Progressive who hissed so hard a second time snot flew out his nose.

Listen, I said with some heat, hiss all you like. But in Western Kentucky there's this big coal-digging machine, three stories tall, with JAWS, man, that eats whole truckloads of ground at a bite. It's got legs! It WALKS, man, for twenty years it's been walking on this certain piece of ground, around and around, eating dirt and scooping up coal to heat and light the nation. Gradually the machine has dug a hole three-hundred feet deep and a quarter-mile square around the rims of its pit. And after twenty years, the coal is gone and the machine itself is done for. Parts worn, design obsolete, there it sits at the bottom of its pit, and they can't get it out! It would cost the company more than the thing is worth to dismantle it and take it out so what's the company going to do? Leave it there, that's what. Bury it where it quit. Think about it!

BULLSHIT! shouted Jay the ex-Progressive. YOU'RE NO DRUNK. YOU'RE AN IMPOSTER. YOU'RE A GODDAMN NUTCASE!

Oh, I'm a drunk all right, I said to Jay. And a neurotic and a depressive and a solitary and brooding self-indulgent failure, just as my girlfriend Gretchen said. And I may be a nutcase too. I don't want to justify myself or try to appear to anyone in any winning light. I know I'm not a pretty sight to look at and my recent personal victories have been minor ones. But small as they may be, they are actual, I have earned them, I have paid hard dues for them and I will NOT anymore apologize for any information that flows through me. Hiss if you want to. But listen: not three months ago, the government issued a call for someone in this country to write a myth for the nation, to be read by the people of future ages, a story, to be inserted, planted, as it were, like a seed in the public consciousness, that it might take root and be told in oral transmission for centuries, a story that will explain the nuclear dumps to people and make their presence and their dangers known in a way that no system of physical signs could ever be depended upon to stay posted and convey the word for the thousands of years required.

102

Poor government. Poor sad public and its representatives, bereft of all art, legend, lore. I wrote to the government, I told it about the Toyota plant standing on the ground where the ancient bison fed, about the Shawnee and the Cherokee hunting there, and Boone, and the legend of the Bluegrass as an Eden. Here is your myth, I told the government. And I will tell more.

NUTCASE! screamed Jay the ex-Progressive.

I don't see where any of this can lead or what Helen hopes to achieve. As much as I like Helen she frustrates me sometimes. Quite often in fact. I guess this is all meant to do me some good. "Guide us through the wilderness," were Dorothy's words. What if I enjoy the damn wilderness? What if the wilderness is where I am trying to get to? I'm not saying I am, but I'm not as frantic in it as I once was. I could live well in the wilderness if I had to. But, on we must go, says Helen. Trudge trudge trudge.

Between what we think and what we are able to say, what we see in our mind's eye, and the words we find to speak about it: language, mental process. Here at Bluegrass Clinic we ponder such things, in the evenings, early mornings, and during the breaks between sessions. Sometimes we ponder them during the sessions. No holds barred is Helen's motto.

Narrative Therapy

LET ME HAVE your attention please," said Helen. "I'd like you all to find a place on the floor and get comfortable. Use the cushions and pillows anyway you like. Put a little space between yourselves, a comfortable place that is your own, where you can rest and relax and feel very contented. Fix your pillows, get them under you and around you in some way that makes you cozy. Now stretch out, full length, really stretch, and begin to take nice, deep breaths. Continue to breathe and as you breathe, bring your attention here, where we are. Be in this room, be with your body as it stretches and relaxes on the floor. All those loose items rattling around in your mind, gather them up and bring them to the front of your attention, then release them to float away. We want to be where we are, fully and restfully, we want to be present. The rest of the world is somewhere else, doing what it wants to do. We're here doing what we want to do. Be at peace in your body and your spirit. Don't think, don't not-think. Good. We're all here together in this quiet time and place. Keep your eyes closed. I'm going to ask Dorothy to say what is on her mind just now. What do you see, Dorothy?"

"I see a line of taxis outside an airport," said Dorothy.

"Thank you. We may want to hire one of those taxis in a little while to take us someplace. A few of you laughed a little at Dorothy's taxis, that's okay. Don't censor your thoughts. It's okay to chuckle a little if you do it quietly. But please don't allow your response to intrude on anyone else's response. Good, thank you. Breathe in and out slowly, breathe deeply. Keep your eyes closed, everyone, and I'll ask Gordon what he sees in his mind's eye just now. Gordon?"

"I see a bunch of guys playing basketball," said Gordon.

"Are you in the game with them?"

"Yeah, I'm in it. There's guys all around me, playing basketball."

"Thank you, Gordon. Charlotte, tell us what your picture is about now?"

"My pictures are all jumping around."

"Can you make out anything?"

"Yeah, I'm petting a cat. I'm sitting on the floor, petting a big gray cat. The grownups are on the chairs and in the swing talking. We're all out on the porch."

"Are you happy on the porch?"

"Oh yes, I like it very much."

"You stay there and enjoy it, Charlotte, while I ask Wilgus what kind of pictures he sees."

"I see my father in the Veterans Hospital," said Wilgus. "He looks very sad."

"Are you in the picture with him?"

"I'm close by, looking at him, but I can't see myself."

"Do you want to see yourself there with your father?"

"Not really. I'm okay on the sidelines."

"Where exactly is your father sitting, Wilgus? Is he sitting?"

"Yeah, he's sitting on his bunk, smoking a cigarette and looking at a magazine."

"What are you thinking?"

"It's weird. I'm thinking about the U.S. Army. My dad was in the

Army and I was in the Army for six months in 1961. And I think: there's been a hundred percent turnover in the U.S. Army since I was a soldier. I showed up at Fort Benning, Georgia, and the Army had, let's say, a million men in it, thanks to President Eisenhower's universal training program in which all American males would receive six months of active duty military training followed by eight years in the ready reserve. Then the Vietnam War came and went and all the conflicts, engagements, and military missions of the seventies and eighties came and went and in those years the U.S. Army turned itself over, personnel-wise, one-hundred percent. What that means in plain English is that there's not one dude left in that whole big system that was in it when I was there in the early 1960s! Yet it's still the same Army."

"I DON'T FIND THIS TALK VERY INTERESTING AT ALL," said Jay.

"Wilgus is not under any obligation to entertain you," said Anita. "This is his time. He can say anything he wants, just like you did this morning, which quite frankly I didn't think was very interesting myself."

"That's enough," said Helen. "Jay, the point is, try not to be attached to other people's experiences. Can't you see that your attachment to Wilgus's words is a form of addiction?"

"HEARING BULLSHIT IS MY EXPERIENCE," said Jay. "IT HAPPENS TO ME. I DON'T CALL THAT AN ADDICTION."

"Just let Wilgus talk since it is his turn," said Helen. "That's all you need to think about."

"Can I go on now?" asked Wilgus, still with his eyes closed.

"Yes, you were saying about the military. . ."

"I mean, we get in these wars, right? We fight, die, widows and orphans are created but America is so psychologically fractured we can't maintain coherent generational national memory. I was just a kid in World War II but I remember it like it was yesterday, it fills my head. It's hard to believe but the experience of the Vietnam War is already fading from memory, not from the soldiers who fought it but from that amorphous thing we call the nation. We are already forgetting Vietnam, while my own mind will not let go of World War II. My generation has been called 'Hitler's Children' after the World War II movie about Nazi Germany I first saw in 1944."

Wilgus was ready to tell about *Hitler's Children* and all that it meant, but Helen said that was enough for today.

Hitler's Children

TIME IS IN and around us and everywhere at once, and time is eternal and there is no time. The earth spins and revolves around the sun and the centuries pass, yet from the beginning, from the original source of all, time has not skipped a beat. Not one day, not one second of time has been leaped over in the progress of all the centuries. It's been fifteen thousand and so many days since Hitler died in his bunker; we could figure it exactly if we wanted to.

I was living at Grandma's and Granddad's on Trace Fork when Hitler shot himself. President Roosevelt had died only a few weeks before. For young people today, 1945 is ancient history but for me it seems like yesterday. I was personally alive when those world-historic events occurred. I shared life on Planet Earth with Hitler and Roosevelt, Stalin, Mussolini, Tojo and Hirohito, all of us breathing oxygen at the same time, breathing as they breathed.

Now they're all dead, but I'm still here. I have remained alive on this earth all the succeeding moments and hours and days in an unbroken flow of time. During time, oceans have formed and receded, continents have risen from the waters and broken apart. All around the earth this very hour, volcanoes cook and hiss and roar and bleed their fire across the living land. Time has BEEN, all this time, eons leading across the space of years right down to our very own most recent half century in which I have been alive and aware and breathing on this planet.

In the hotel room where I've been living, I've got a big-screen stereo television and a VCR all set up in front of my reclining chair. This whole past year I have sat in that chair eight or ten hours a day, every day, often from three in the afternoon until long after midnight, sipping whiskey and watching movies about the war. I read books and watch programs with considerable interest about any war. But it's the old pictures of World War II that carry me down to where I really live.

They carry me down into Time, connect me to some old place of truth in the feelings and the psyche so compelling I want to live there. I know I can't live there, and that it's unhealthy to even want to, and I know that is why I am here now talking to you about these things. I know I can't go on sitting in my chair watching TV forever but for the last year, that's about all I've been doing: *Victory at Sea* and *The Gallant Years* and *Why We Fight* and *Between the Wars* and *Air Power* and *Sands of Iwo Jima* and *Gung Ho!* and *Wake Island* and *Corregidor* and *To Hell and Back* and *Battleground* and *The Nazis Strike* and *Blitzkrieg* and *Thirty Seconds over Tokyo* and *Hitler's Children*.

Most of the film is combat photography showing the fighting around the world, the Eastern Front, the Western Front, the South Pacific, the Philippines, North Africa, Sicily, Italy, reel after reel of soldiers marching, navies at sea, pictures of tanks, planes, ships, artillery, invasions, paratroop landings, amphibious landings, jungle fighting, desert fighting, mountain war, war on the beaches, in the bombed-out cities of Russia and Poland and France and England and Germany and a hundred other countries.

Hour after hour I show these pictures to myself and sip my whiskey and let it carry me down and down, back through time.

What pictures I can't find on television to copy, I order from the video clubs. I belong to two military video clubs; they each send me a new cassette about the war every month. *The Fighting Seabees. The Flying Tigers. From the Halls of Montezuma.* Listen, back in those old war years I used to sit with my grandfather in the kitchen at the homeplace and listen to the war news with him. He had four sons in the war. One son, my Uncle Wayne whom I never knew, had already been killed in the Philippines in the first year of the war, when I was only two. My father fought in southern Italy in the winter and spring of 1944. My Uncle Delmer fought all across France, the Rhine River. My Uncle Junior was on Okinawa getting ready to invade Japan when the war ended.

And there Grandma and Granddad were at home, going on with their lives and there I was with them, calling their house my home. Every morning Granddad got up at four to catch the work bus to Black Oak Mine where he would work all day underground. Then in the evenings after his bath and after supper he'd sit by the radio listening to the news and I would sit there with him. Hearing the news from around the world, sometimes listening to the actual sounds of battles from the front line correspondents, it was as if we were THERE, far away, around the world, members of the world community.

I was only five in 1944 but I felt very much a member of the nation and the world. I was part of the war effort for my country, part of World Reality. In a sense, I haven't felt in reality since that time. Life has been a kind of dream, a dream I am not entirely free of to this day. As a child in those war years, I felt absolutely in reality. I was a citizen of the United States of America and a patriotic one at that, hard at work, doing my bit, part of the effort, fighting the fascists. My father was fighting. My uncles were fighting. My grandparents were working hard in the mines and on the farm.

My job was to collect scrap iron from the neighbors up and down Trace Fork, and then to participate in parades and war bond rallies in town on Saturdays. Every week I went up and down the creek knocking on people's doors and asking them to put their scrap iron on the pile I had going outside my Great-aunt Frony's store at the mouth of the creek. Pots and pans, curtain rods, coat hangers, old chains, tin roofing, hub caps, toothpaste tubes, anything metal. In town I would ride on the floats in the parades and march with the school children in the war bond rallies. I even performed a few times at some of the smaller rallies outside Aunt Frony's store. I'd get up on a truck bed with this little toy guitar someone had given me and I would beat the hell out of that thing and sing "You Are My Sunshine" and "Home on the Range" and "God Bless America," trying to sell war bonds to the people.

On Sundays we'd go into town to see the free war movies at the theater. The streets in town would be packed with people. The theater would be packed. All afternoon the theater would fill and empty and fill again for the war films they were showing, *The Battle of Britain, The Rape of Nanking, The March of Time.* I saw *Hitler's Children* at the Kentucky Theater on Main Street in Blaine, Kentucky, in 1944. I watched the children being devoured by the fascists before my very eyes. Then forty some years of unbroken time went by and I didn't see or even think about *Hitler's Children.* Now I have my own copy of it in my hotel room and I watch it two or three times a week along with all the rest. I'd be home watching it now, reaching into time, plumbing time, diving into time's dark ocean in search of the sunken wrecks if Helen hadn't told me that I need to join you in this circle.

Sandplay

THE SAND TABLE where Wilgus and Beth Ann worked was about the size of a billiard table, with walls around the sides eight inches high. The table was divided across the middle by a partition. White sand six inches deep covered both ends of the table. The wall behind the table was covered by shelves with an assortment of dolls and toy figures: nuns, priests, cowboys, soldiers, aviators, hunters, miners, farmers, young brides, seductive whores, old wise women, sitting Buddhas, angels, horses, cows, dogs, sheep, lions, tigers, elephants, wolves, plastic barns, houses, churches, schools, street lamps, plastic trees, rocks, small archetypal figures carved from wood, chiseled in stone, rendered in glass and metal and ceramic.

Wilgus spent the first hour creating two large mountains of sand, then covering them with dozens of small plastic trees and ferns and green fronds to create a jungle. To make an ocean he scooped a depression in the right front corner of the table, then filled it with water from a pitcher. Between the ocean and the mountains Wilgus arranged several tiny plastic houses around a church, a hotel, a post office and a school building to form a town. Behind the highest hill Wilgus nestled a green ceramic Buddha four inches high in a grove of trees and tall ferns so dense the Buddha was nearly hidden from view. To the left of Buddha Wilgus placed a large Bengal tiger with its mouth open wide, ready to pounce.

Wilgus stepped back to survey the little world he had created. With his eyes he searched the shelves filled with figurines. After handling several of them he chose a figure of a young hunter with a deer slung over his shoulders. He stood the hunter in front of the church, then beside him set a figure of a young woman in a white wedding dress, complete with veil. He was working rapidly now, his hands no longer hesitating to pluck items from the shelves and add them to his sand tray tableau. He found a wooden bridge the size of his hand and set it over a narrow blue plastic river that flowed languidly past the town. Spotting a three-inch zinc Lone Ranger with pistol at the ready, Wilgus seized it from the shelf and boldly stood it at water's edge like a masked amphibian emerging from the sea.

By now Wilgus was grinning like a child in a free, pure spirit of play. Maybe the Lone Ranger would invade the town and kidnap the bride from the hunter. Maybe they would flee together and run into the mountains where the tiger and the Buddha waited. Scenarios flashed in his mind like movie scenes but Wilgus ignored them and worked on with his hands. His hands knew what to do. Swiftly they grabbed new figures from the shelves and placed them in the tableau unfolding in the sand. From a basket he took five tiny ceramic baby ducks and arranged them on the blue river.

As he set a fisherman holding a pole at the water's edge his hand accidentally struck the Lone Ranger and knocked him face-down in the sand. There are no accidents in the universe, said Helen. Without a pause Wilgus plucked a miniature whiskey bottle from another basket filled with tiny objects and placed it on the sand next to the Lone Ranger's gun-hand. Perfect. As fast as his right hand could pluck more bottles from the basket his left hand scattered them around the supine masked man. From the same basket he took several miniature beer cans and scattered them in the sand as well.

114

Finally he picked up both small baskets and emptied them onto the sand all around the unconscious half-drowned Lone Ranger.

Beth Ann spent her first half-hour as a Sandplay artist creating a small village of wooden houses along two intersecting streets, lined with trees. At the intersection she placed two churches, a school and a courthouse. Behind the village she created a forest consisting of twenty plastic cedar trees. As she pondered her village scene she held a hand-carved painted figure of the Madonna. From a shelf covered with toy vehicles of all kinds she took a huge truck and laid it on its side in the middle of the intersection. With both hands she scooped up a dozen automobiles and crashed them on all sides of the truck.

With yet more scoops she extended the carnage until the streets were filled with wrecked vehicles of all kinds, piled on top of each other. For the rest of the hour she added wrecked vehicles to all four lines of traffic. Gradually the wreckage extended beyond the town's limits, out into the desert, until the lines of crashed vehicles touched the edges of the sand table. After a pause, she began to draw a circle in the sand around the town and its lines of crashed cars. The sand table was a canvas, Beth Ann the artist, arranging elements of a story she did not know she knew.

"This is beautiful, Beth Ann," said Helen. "You've made a perfect mandala."

During the mid-morning break from the Sandplay session Beth Ann asked Wilgus, "How come you're so nervous?"

"What do you mean?" said Wilgus.

"You just seem like a nervous guy. Uptight."

"Why do you think that?" asked Wilgus nervously. Wilgus was thirty years older than Beth Ann but the young woman's assertiveness intimidated him.

"Just by the way you carry yourself. You act like you want to apologize for being alive."

The young woman's forehead had turned red but when Wilgus looked into her eyes he found no messages in them. Finally he said, "This is a strange conversation."

"This is a strange therapeutic situation we're in," Beth said.

Wilgus looked on in total suspense, the figures on his side of the table forgotten. Their exchange left him furious but strangely enlivened. Why had the presiding shrink at Bluegrass Clinic partnered a fifty-three-year-old alcoholic newspaperman with a twenty-two-year-old schizophrenic in such a risky symbolic archetype game as Sandplay? What did Helen want Wilgus and Beth Ann to discover, what insight or life lesson did she mean for them to find? Had Helen instructed this young woman to say the things to him she had just said, intending to produce the reaction he was feeling now?

On Wednesday of his third week at Bluegrass Clinic, Wilgus woke up feeling so weak he couldn't get out of bed. Through the window by his bedside he watched the zebras cavorting in the savanna. Delta. Mudflats. Rhinos. Beyond the zebras at the water's edge two Great Blue Herons rose from their perches on a gnarly Marula tree and flew away into the dawn now breaking in the eastern sky. Unable to sleep, he stood in front of the bathroom mirror at three a.m. trying to find his mother's face in his own. When he was young, people who had known his mother often told him that he looked just like her. Alice had been a slender person and so had Wilgus until he was nearly thirty. This always pleased him.

People said his mother was a crazy woman. Aunt Jenny said, Wilgus, your mother is not crazy, she's very wounded is all.

What wounded her? Wilgus asked.

Just life, said Aunt Jenny.

Wilgus's first awarenesses of life were that his mother was going away. Being taken away. He remembers it clearly, the entire scene brilliant in his mind forty years later. His uncle, his grandmother, a taxi driver and a deputy sheriff wrestling his mother into the grim gray Oldsmobile coupe with a taxi sign over the windshield. Fighting his mother into the car. Wilgus watching from across the yard, standing with his aunt, both of them witnesses. It took half an hour to get his mother into that car. They got her in then because she got too tired to fight anymore. They wore her down, then put her in the back seat and the deputy got in beside her and the uncle got in the front and they drove off down the creek and a year went by.

The hairs on my head are turning gray. Should I dye it? Wear a hat? I need to get my driver's license back and hit the road for some big city, leaving all here behind. Disappear.

Hypothermia

HYPOTHERMIA can strike without warning. Hypothermia is a sudden reduction of body temperature. It freezes you to the core. The usual cause of hypothermia is overexposure to conditions that reduce your body temperature to an unnatural degree. Homeless alcoholics are in grave danger of hypothermia in wintertime, so try to not be homeless or an alcoholic. When you are getting hypothermia, you begin to shiver. If your body temperature gets down to 95 degrees Fahrenheit, you will definitely shiver. If your body gets below 90 degrees Fahrenheit, you can't think straight. When it gets below 80 degrees Fahrenheit, you are in deep doo-doo. Your heart will slow down and you may enter a coma. Many people live their entire lives in comas and don't even know it; they have a form of emotional hypothermia. If you are suffering from hypothermia, the best thing you can do is get under a pile of wool blankets with a good friend and stay there 'til your body temperature returns to normal.

Questionnaire

ARE YOU CURRENTLY in a state of transition or change? Do you find you have difficulty letting go of past attachments and starting new beginnings? Do you often experience fatigue, lassitude, passivity and not know why? Are you obsessed by the past? Does depression surround you like a cloud? Have there been past traumas or shocks in your life that you ain't got over yet? Are you monstrously scarred by a traumatic early-life relationship with your father? Mother? Both? How many sets of people have you run through? Do you drink alcoholic depressants and then wonder why you are depressed? Have you suffered personal losses that you can't get over? Are you the kind of jerk who prepares your exit from relationships even as a relationship begins? Do you suffer from mental anguish and deep despair? Are you troubled by nightmares? Have you grown a second head without realizing it and appear to others as a hideous beast? Do you make the same mistake over and over again? Do you feel that life is passing you by? Do you sit alone in your room watching television, drinking bourbon and writing notes to yourself? Do you give in to the demands of other people just to avoid an argument? How far is it to Baltimore? What about hypothermia?

Welcome to New York

It WAS PEGGY who gave me that speed to take to Don and Mona in New York that time, the fall of '68, after Chicago. I was supposed to stay with Don and Mona but for some reason they weren't there when I arrived, we'd got our signals crossed somehow. I was two days early or they were two days late getting back from South America or California or Morocco or wherever they'd been. In those days I didn't know a soul in New York except them. If I'd had a return bus ticket I'd probably have gone on back to Chicago but I didn't. All I had was my jacket and satchel and twenty-three dollars and this bottle of Benzedrine pills Peggy was sending to Don and Mona to pay them back for some old deal of a couple of years ago before I knew any of these people. So with two days to kill I decided to make the best of the situation and began eating Peggy's bennies and doing things like going to movies and riding the subway and sitting around in coffee shops to amuse myself and pass the time.

By evening of the first day I'd established a routine that pleased me very much; it intrigued me, like a mystery. I was glad to be alone in New York, disconnected from personal time or history. There was a movie theater in Times Square showing *Juliet of the Spirits* and 8 1/2 as a double feature. I'd never seen a Fellini film before, so I took another of Peggy's pills and went to see these movies in the late afternoon and when I came out I rode the subway to the Battery and caught the ferry over to Staten Island and then back. The ferry only cost a nickel in those days, and the round trip took an hour, a wonderful hour of fresh air and water and visual splendor, the Statue of Liberty going out and then the evening lights of Manhattan on the return. I rode the subway back to Times Square and bought a newspaper and went into a little grill and had chili and coffee and a piece of pie while I read the paper and rested and looked around at the people. The chili only cost sixty cents, the pie was fifty, the coffee a quarter, the subway twenty cents and the movie less than a dollar. I saw how I could live well for two days on Benzedrine and twenty dollars if I stuck to my route that I'd blazed that first afternoon in the city.

Sometime soon after dark I took more speed and went back to the theater and saw *Juliet of the Spirits* and 8½ again, then took the subway back to the Battery and again rode the ferry to Staten Island and back, and then rode the subway back to Times Square to my little grill again where I felt very much like a regular by now. I felt like a regular in all of New York. I'd discovered my place there. I had a role that was hugely pleasing to me because every time I made my rounds again I went deeper into it, further down into a mystery that I tried to tell this lady about in the Metropolitan Museum after losing all count of how many bennies I'd taken or how many times I'd been on the ferry or seen *Juliet* or 8½ or had coffee and chili and pie and read the paper in the café. Surely I'd enacted the total ritual four or five times. I varied my rounds only once, the second night, when perhaps out of slight boredom and the beginnings of fatigue and the warning signs of depression I decided to set out walking from the Battery toward Brooklyn Bridge. I didn't even have a map of the streets. I was going by feel.

124

I'd been thinking about Brooklyn Bridge ever since my student days when I discovered Whitman and Crane and Thomas Wolfe and Kerouac. I walked through the dark and no doubt dangerous streets but no harm came to me.

Even though I was feeling the first ragged edges of my coming collapse the city seemed abundant in its blessings. Absolutely to my surprise at four in the morning I came upon Fulton Fish Market. After walking the darkened streets near the waterfront, suddenly there was this enormous lit-up place where hundreds of people were cutting and packing fish, tons of fish, millions of fish just off the boats from the Atlantic Ocean, the day's catch being prepared for the day's consumption by ten million people of a city. And they made me welcome. The workers allowed me in. They seemed glad to see me. Hey Mac, what're you doing out so early? Hey Mac, where you going? Teasing me. I was an oddity to them. Just walking, I told them. What is this place? It's the Fulton Fish Market, they answered proudly.

I tried to explain it all to the lady in the museum. I got on a talking jag with her. With the last of my good energy before my fall, I wanted to tell somebody about my experience the past few days, the past few years, and this nice lady, a young and well-dressed woman, seemed willing to listen although she said not a word to me. I told her about my days in the city, about the subway and the ferry and Fellini and the million fish, the shad, the squid, the bass, the roe, and the workers who were packing and shipping. I told her about the bridge, about walking on it as the sun came up before the traffic, about Whitman and Wolfe and Crane. Then stories about my family in Kentucky started spilling out, right there in the museum, portraits and statues and suits of armor all around. It felt so great, that the well-dressed lady was willing to listen, that she

125

wasn't afraid of me. I knew I looked pretty wild-eyed and scruffy after two days without a shave or bath, but she knew I meant no harm, she knew I was on an adventure and that it was urgent that I talk. I've got this grandfather, I told her. Old Granddad Collier on Trace Fork, in Kentucky, in the coalfields in Finley County. My grandfather was a miner forty years before he retired, I told her. Before that he was a logger, from Floyd County. My father and all my uncles were miners. Grandma Collier herself is a farmer, she works a thirty-acre hillside at the head of Trace Fork, on the north side of Balsam Ridge. She milks two cows twice a day, she raises hogs and chickens and guinea hens. Every Saturday she wrings the necks of four big frying chickens and pulls their heads off with her hands and then plucks them and cleans them for Sunday dinner. Every summer with her own hands she raises enough food for the family to live a whole year nearly. Every fall she shoots two big hogs in the head with her .22 and guts them with a knife and carves them up and dresses them out. She cooks the whole head down to make her souse. When she cuts up cabbage to make her kraut and chow-chow her tool is a number ten can filed razor sharp all around its circular edge. Every Monday she works eight hours washing clothes for the family, then spends most of Tuesday ironing them. At least in the old days she worked that hard. She's older now, I told the woman, she doesn't do as much.

I must have talked to the lady an hour or more, until finally at last a man in a suit came up and took her by the arm to lead her away. But before they left the man held out his hand to me and said his name. He spoke with an accent. He was Polish. He worked for the United Nations, he said. The lady was his fiancé, in New York for a visit. She had no English, he explained. But both appreciated my courtesy to her. They smiled. I was too flabbergasted to smile back but we did shake hands again, the lady too this time. I was coming down hard by now. All I could think to say as we parted was, welcome to New York.

The Dream

SLEEPING BY THE RIVER I dreamed a snake was coiled up in me. I felt it move in my chest and guts, I felt it crawl up my throat and out my mouth and across my face. I saw it move across the rock shelf to the water. I saw it swim across the water into the woods on the other side.

And I dreamed that a young doe came up to me in the woods and motioned for me to follow her. It was dark and a rain was falling but I followed behind until we came to a laurel dell at the base of a rock cliff where a young buck stood, waiting. The doe touched his neck with her nose and the buck nodded and fell in behind us walking.

We walked until we came to a river ford. The doe said, kill this buck and skin it and put on its hide. I killed the buck with my knife and skinned it. I put on his hide like a cloak and with the doe walked into the night until we came to the top of a hill. We stood together looking at the moon, letting it shine upon us, until the hill became a rim of a crater on the moon, and I was alone upon it.

I lay down and slept. I dreamed I stood inside a crater of the moon. I stepped into a hole in the center of the crater and fell through the dark so swiftly I woke up alone in a cave, lying on my back, gazing through the smoke hole at the full bright moon in the sky. I felt the warm ashes in the fireplace. A few embers were still alive. Soon I had a new fire. I sat a long time looking into the flames. The flames are like the sun, I thought. And when I thought of the sun I thought of the moon and I looked up through the smoke hole but the earth had turned and the moon had passed from view.

I hated to leave my fire but I did without looking back. I walked out of the cave among the rocks that led to the river bank. The moon lit the water silver. The river was a streak of light playing in the gorge. I walked across the water on the rocks, then climbed the cliffs until I got to the top where the pines were short and scrubby, not much taller than me. I could see the full moon clear from there, straight above, round as a pumpkin, shining the purest light I'd ever seen. It fell across me, across the whole plateau of pine, it lit the far horizon of the hills, it fell into the gorge making shadows on the cliffs that I had climbed.

The gorge was illumined, showered upon and shadowed by the full clear fall of light. The gorge was a crater. In the moonlight I walked down the crater's side, circling, doubling back until I reached the bottom, the center of the bottom, reached the opening. Without hesitation I stepped into it and fell until I woke again beside the remnants of my fire. The ashes were still warm. With both hands I scooped up ashes and pressed them against me. I pressed them warm between my legs, into my belly, I rubbed their heat into my flesh, down each thigh to my knees, then with more ash down both legs to my feet. I placed my feet in the pile of ashes, buried them deep while I rubbed my chest and neck and face and arms with the soft warm ash of burned wood.

When I was covered and warmed all over I stood and walked around my cave, wearing the ash like clothes. But I longed for the water and soon I was among the rocks by the water's edge again. I stood beside a long, deep pool looking at my image in the water, reflecting silver in the moonlight. I couldn't see my face but I saw my shape clearly and the shine of the ash on my skin. I recognized the shape of the figure in the water as my own. But the figure was a stranger, too, a woman. When I lifted my hand she lifted hers. I began to dance with this woman of the water, I moved on the rocky shore while she moved with me in the water. I raised my hand. She raised her hand. I shifted my feet and turned. The woman turned. I bowed low and most elegantly, and she bowed, too, our faces nearly touching. I brought my arms around in a swoop and she did, too, until our hands were nearly touching.

Then my hands sank into the water to the wrists; instantly the ash washed away and my hands drew my entire body into the water. I plunged head first into the pool and swam, down, reaching deep, turning over and over in the cold river. The ash washed off like dust. I turned in the water, I turned again, I was a fish. The water was my habitat, I lay suspended in it, running my hands over my body, feeling my own flesh, delighting in it. I looked around for the woman I had seen in the water. I swam deeper and searched along the ledges but she was not there. I looked up but all I could see above was the wavy round light of the moon.

I swam toward it, reaching for the surface. I pulled through the water toward the bright image of the moon, up, toward the surface and the warm air of the night. But the longer I swam the colder the water became, and I realized I was swimming down, the moon was down. The water grew colder and colder as I went deeper. For the first time I did not feel at home within the deep. But as soon as the small fear hit me, the woman of the water appeared beside me and touched me with her hand. She swam in front of me and held my face in her two hands, pulling me close. She pressed her mouth against mine, she wrapped her legs around my legs, she held me

131

tightly in her arms while my arms floated freely out to the sides. Kicking gently, we swam slowly together, down, deep toward the shining moon. We approached the moon. Its light was brilliant, yet comforting to the eyes. We could see its craters, its hills and plains and valleys spread out before us as we swam entwined through the brilliant water. Our motion carried us to the rim of a crater on the moon, and past it, down, over the rocks and crags of its side to the bottom where a hole lay open before us. Come, it said. Fall. Swim through to the other side.

Quilt Thread

SLOWLY THE SHINING OBJECT rises through the water.
Trying to get to the core of something these few remaining days.

Sets of words buried in ancient matter.

Sunlight strikes the edges, first hint of definition.

The lake shore is barren but in the distance a small stream flows
into the lake through a copse of willow trees.

But where does the stream begin? Where are the headwaters?

Pattern of the tributaries.

People recognize me as I walk by, they nod and wave, mouthing
words of greeting I cannot hear. I know as time goes by I am less
substantial as a corporeal body. A certain floating quality hovers
behind the "known" world.

Sweet people of bygone times smile as they say goodbye. Oh
please don't go, I say, stay a while longer.

This way, says the voice of a child. A small boy motions for me
to follow. I walk behind him through a narrow passageway that
leads to higher ground.

A hundred years ago my grandmother played in this creek. It
meant to her what it meant to my father and then to me. Spaces
in a meta-narrative, room in the mind to wander. Unset the stone.
Impossibility of knowing mind. Floating contents. A million frozen
moments inside the cave, behind the cliffs the ice age still goes on,

frozen scenes embedded in the ceiling, the walls melt down flood time freeing of the waters.

What could organize the billion images and their projections? All the people I have known, every place I've lived, places I have seen, breathed, walked upon, desert resting places, camping spots, certain hot springs in the Cascades, remote waterfalls, cold pools in the high Sierras, deep in the canyons of the Santa Cruz range, Deep Creek in the Blue Ridge, Powell Valley, Cane Creek, Trace Fork in Kentucky before the strip mining.

I confess my conceit in thinking that all meanings can be conveyed by words.

Poetry. Victory of haiku.

There goes old John Stepp, headed to the Post Office. John writes plays for the local stage. My father worked with John on the tipple at Black Gold before the war, they knew each other well. I've got a picture of him standing next to my father who has his arm around my mother who is holding me. My parents are young and sweet-looking. The worst hasn't hit 'em yet. Soul-crushing blindside slam against the fate-wall, everyone you know and love ground up, overwhelming forces, gone.

So much sadness everywhere, it's like fog or weather, ever present everywhere all the time for years.

When the war ended, my dad used to go on these long lonesome job hunts with twenty dollars in his pocket that his father had loaned him, riding the Greyhound bus all night to Terre Haute, Michigan City, Akron, Cleveland, Cincinnati, arriving at dawn to start a new round of job hunting. Bus stations were elaborate facilities in those days, small towns in themselves. He lived in bus stations on his trips, slept in them sitting up many times, eggs, toast, coffee, cigarettes, terminal cafés. He would set out early in the morning to call on the factories, warehouses, stockyards, employment offices, where he had left his applications on previous trips. Then go around to other factories and fill out more applications, janitor jobs in office buildings, school buildings, government buildings, hospitals.

Before the war my dad worked in the pony mines around home. For a while in the Allais mine. In Italy in 1944, he led pack mules up the mountains hauling food and water and ammunition and on the way back down carried out the dead and bloody wounded. Sometimes even mules couldn't get to where the fighting was and men like my dad carried rations and ammunition up the steep hillsides on pack boards strapped to their backs, then by hand hauled the dead and injured down to the waiting mules.

After the war my dad was permanently tired. I still see him in his laid-off years, walking up the creek carrying on his shoulder a box of groceries bought on credit at the commissary, dark hair slicked back from his forehead, sad shadowed face, open innocent startled look he wore most of the time, accepting of his fate. My father wasn't innocent or naïve about life, he was too near death to act as if he didn't know the darker secrets. No, it was more that he was resigned, resigned to having no proper suitcase, what's wrong with carrying one's traveling things in a cardboard box held shut by binder's twine?

I knew that my father was depressed, that he felt defeated, that his life was a life of pain. I wanted so much to help him, reassure him, tell him that it was okay, certainly that I was okay. He had no way of getting any money, he never had any in his pockets but in my kid world I always had plenty of money. I had piggy banks and savings accounts and little sums that came in from my aunts and uncles. One time my dad was out of cigarettes and I knew he wanted them and needed them but he had no money and he was sitting around the house in nicotine withdrawal, not complaining or calling attention to his problem. Everyone else around, my grandparents and aunts and uncles coming and going, were too busy in their lives to notice my dad was suffering. He didn't have twenty cents to buy a pack of Camels while I had dollars in various stashes hidden away in my secret places, money I'd saved, coins I'd found under cushions on the couch and chairs. I knew he wouldn't accept any of my money so I pretended to find some in a drawer of one of the end tables in the living room. Look here, I said, holding up a fifty-cent piece from the open drawer and we set out walking down the creek together to the store. He had to stop and rest several times. My gentle father doing his best.

Daddy, I remember you, I remember your sad brown eyes looking out from under your bushy eyebrows. I remember tears from your eyes running down your cheeks. I remember you smiling. I remember you laughing the day I visited you in the VA hospital. I hadn't seen you in two whole years. We wrote letters, you kept my letters. I kept yours the best I could.

Face-down in dark water, the shining object rises through the fathoms toward the light. Snow falling through the trees, Red Knight waiting, silent snowy trees. Age four, one whole afternoon, Mother teaching me to dance, my great love holding both my hands leading me across the kitchen floor to the music. I can dance! We twirl about and laugh. I'm lifted up, through the air I fly. Then she holds me against her body, my face pressed to her neck, my legs around her waist. Mother holds my hand as we wade across the river. We are going to a sandy beach on the other side to have a picnic. The water covers my ankles, the water covers my knees, the water is over my head, I can't breathe. The water flows in a narrow channel and my foot goes down in a step-off hole and I go underwater and lose my mother's hand and the water washes me away. I come up and through the water I see my mother, her strong legs running toward me. I go under the water again. And then my mother lifts me up in the daylight and I am saved.

Electricity through the brain. They say it doesn't hurt, doesn't take long, I doubt anybody ever gets used to it. In twelve years my mom had twenty-seven shock treatments. When I was eleven, I dreamed I broke into the hospital and snuck her out and drove her to Oregon and got a job with the Forest Service as a lookout. She said, son, we should go back to Kentucky, it would be the right thing to do. Surreal Kentucky. Eastern Kentucky, in strike time, welfare lines, mine violence, men swarming everywhere, carrying guns, talking, hanging around in bunches, gathering at the commissary.

Fifty cars going up Sand Lick Mountain in the night, the road winding up the hill, at the scenic overlook you could see the whole thing at once. Two miles long, strung out on the road, the tail lights of the cars looked like a piece of string on fire. By four a.m. a hundred people on the picket line in front of the non-union mine, people standing and talking to each other while two dozen young State Police troopers lean on the sides of their police cars, also talking casually amongst themselves. The regular mine workers arrive at six a.m., their vehicles appear from the still-darkened road, the pickets bunch up tightly in front of the mine gate, the State Police form a straight line, chamber shells into their shotguns, hold the guns at port arms. The scene unfolds the same as previous mornings, the past four days this same ritual, the miners who have arrived to begin their shift wait in their vehicles for the situation to sort itself out.

Surreal Kentucky. Old guys hanging around the commissary, crippled miners that didn't work anymore, playing cards, sipping whiskey, women nursing their babies as they shopped, boys playing mumblety-peg with pocket knives by the railroad tracks. The rawness of coal camp life. We didn't have the modern America sheen, the glaze, the shiny bright-lit neon across the surface of reality the way we do today, before TV and the four-lane roads and malls and shopping centers, our world had a grainy black and white feel, literally, as the trains transported coal, dug out of the ground in huge blocks, coal dust on the surfaces, in the air, that certain burning coal smell that we all loved as we realized when we didn't have it anymore. Coal gons groaning jerking clanging as they tug each other one by one rolling down the tracks from the tipple past the stack of ties the rough boys dared me to climb but I wouldn't, not because I was afraid but because my mother told me not to. I knew it was all dangerous the day they carried a miner from the mine entrance on a stretcher his arm mangled, chest crushed like a rag doll. He was already dead, the first dead person I ever saw.

Stream of consciousness freedom of the spiral journey, it's like jazz, organic form growing out of the thing itself, one thing leading to another, but gently, perhaps energetically, gracefully, water on stone. Information is not facts only. A field of daisies is information, biscuits baking in a coal-stove oven is information. In Italy I hiked up the great hill to Monte Cassino where the bones of St. Benedict survived the American bombing in 1944.

Main Street of Blaine, these storefronts in which I see myself, going down this street that runs through my life and mind and heart like a river. I don't look too bad. Ran into Ruby Wheeler today, we stopped and talked a few minutes. We're always restless around each other in public. Sweet, sad private connection, forever ending. Oh the secrets of our town, unknown and known.

I am lost and alone, floating, I am floating on the highway always between the places where other people are, always between the old days and the new days yet to come. It's a hole, a dark gap filled with wind. Dreams are like fissures in the earth, cracks in the mind through which we see underground. I still love the flowing water, still search out the confluences, crawl around under bridges, paddle my boat in unlikely places, float aimlessly. I am of the creeks, rivers, swinging bridges and will be faithful to the end. Now here alone in water floating in a kayak large enough only for me, I dream my dreams. Lazily I paddle in circles, around and around. I go to my usual place in my Kentucky head and watch scenes from my childhood float by. I need the roar of water rushing through my head.

I'm in New York now. I've had a constriction in my throat for a week. Anxiety, I guess, over the bottleneck I'm going through. Leaving Kentucky in a deeper way. My whole life is a series of leavings from Kentucky.

Overload. Mental struggle. All the things and people of life that interest you. Sheer accumulation of sets of people to know and love, be loyal to. Constellations of circles of friends and acquaintances, in flux all life long; other people's lives that fill spaces in my own. Eras. Epochs. Phases. Death of Alice. Death of Glen. Unwritten letters. Unvisited places. What is a human life, anyway? It's some kind of…flicker. It's a breath, and a leisurely look around. It's a little exercise, some talk, some food, a few warm fires. It's a lot of deeds that leave pictures in your mind, a lot of people and trips from place to place, a series of hellos and goodbyes, comings and goings, a list of hugs and kisses and shakings of the hand.

The world gets lonely as the older people who knew your parents when they were young pass on. I'm now the writer of obituaries, keeper of the record. I don't write the news anymore, can't believe in reality long enough to describe it. Sometimes I get into such lowdown numbed-out brain-dead dry-spirit times there ain't nothing to do but go to Ancient Creek to see Aunt Haze, get myself straightened out.

Granddad deeply understood work, work was what you did, physical labor, you figured it out, learned from the elders, developed your skills by doing, applying yourself, hand work, mind and body in accord meaning you were fully alive mind and body as one, took responsibility, it was not a debate, confusion was not accepted, the job was at hand you could see what needed to be done and you did it including getting along with your friends, family, neighbors, you sent the young ones to school, taught them by example, you naturally did the right thing, you were in alignment right relationship to family neighbors community, you live in accord, never greedy, mindful of others, take care of your tools.

Buying ice in the summertime in 50-pound blocks at the ice house in town, having no car hauling it home in a taxi after church on Sundays, the ice in the cellar wrapped in burlap bags, milk and butter sitting next to it. Milking two cows twice a day by hand, cream rises, scooped off and saved, churning butter by hand, the wooden dasher up and down, conversation going on, the children could do it. I remember with pleasure and pride raising the dasher up and down, up and down, gradually feeling the butter form inside the churn.

Canning quarts of vegetables and fruit, keeping chickens for eggs and meat, every Saturday afternoon Grandma wringing the necks of two or three big fryers, preparation for Sunday dinner. Apple trees on the farm, blackberries in abundance in the pasture, even small kids could help with blackberry picking. In late summer cut the corn in the field, one stalk at a time by hand, dry it in fodder shocks. Dig potatoes in late August, store them in holes in the ground beneath some of the shocks to shield them from the rain.

In fall, slaughter one or two big hogs, kill them and dress them out, make sausage, render lard, smoke the hams. Help Grandma string beans, shell peas, hoe corn, thin corn, pick corn, shuck corn and shell corn for the chickens. Peel apples, pears, peaches, and tomatoes, chop up cabbage for kraut and chow-chow. Help with housework, wash dishes, wax floors, and always, every Monday in the summer without fail, help Grandma put out the wash, wringer washing machine, hang clothes on the line. Make lye soap in the big iron kettle outside the wash house, big vats of peach butter from the peach orchard in the new ground. Out through the woods to the pasture in early mornings and evenings, drive cows in for milking.

Build the house and barn and outbuildings by hand, no power tools, use hand saws, cross-cut saws, axes, hammers and nails, a level, square, lay the house foundation with native stones. Dig wells by hand, lay brick for chimneys and indoor fireplaces, heat by coal fires in grates in two rooms. Running water in the kitchen gravity-fed from the cistern, no other plumbing until after the war. Bring in coal and kindling at night for the morning fires, carry out ashes from grates and kitchen coal stove. On leisurely days bottom chairs with bark stripped from trees. In the evenings, pitch horseshoes, play hide 'n' seek, play checkers.

No car, refrigerator or indoor bathroom, but a party-line telephone, our ring one long and two shorts. After supper, gather around the big floor-model radio in the kitchen, news of the world and entertainment that enlivened our imaginations, Granddad stomping on the floor to stop the static in the radio. Power of radio dramas to create pictures in our minds, spoken words coming through the airwaves spark our imaginations, we are co-creators of the story. I did not see television as a regular thing until I was twenty. Classical music every Sunday. One Sunday afternoon Granddad telling me a story, suddenly he stops, music on the radio stops, Pearl Harbor has been bombed.

An unseen force guides me to a rocky beach where elegant people lounge in reclining chairs. I expect the basement of the clubhouse to be as elegant below as it is above but it's a derelict place, toilets fouled, water spraying from broken pipes, old books, papers, rags, tools, broken toys piled on low tables only inches above the filthy water in which I stand. Only then do I notice that I am naked. Gratefully I put on trousers and a sweater offered by an attendant who leads me to a wide veranda that overlooks the valley. In the distance I see a school bus going up Trace Fork toward my grandparents' house where I lived as a child. I am middle-aged and gray-haired on a school bus filled with children. Slowly the bus climbs the steep hill. Beside the road a swollen creek rushes down the mountain without sound.

This is a moment. Clear and sweet, magical. Sun. Light. Leaves. Green. Life. Air. The breathing life of the world. Quiet. Apples. Moist. So rare, when humans feel themselves in the life of the world. The human capacity to be gently alive in the world, sharing in the breathing, in and out. The language. Words as sound. This is love. One great breathing of all nature, direct experience of unification, ego dissolves, you become the world.

Jack and the Monster

ONE DAY Jack was out in the new ground hoeing corn with his brothers Will and Tom. All at once they heard this racket in the trees and Jack looked around and saw his cousin Vernon running toward him hard as he could run yelling, "Jack, oh Jack, come quick, a monster's loose and eating up everything from here to Kingdom Come."

Vernon ran on up to where Jack and Will and Tom were working and fell over on the ground, huffing and puffing. Finally, when he could talk, he said, "It's the biggest old awful thing that ever was. It breathes smoke and roars like a grizzly bear and it's big as a coal tipple. Made out of iron, got a glass head, it's already captured a man. Keeps him locked up in its head, you can see him in there through that monster's eyes. People on Green Creek's done fled. Mommy sent me to tell you all to run."

"Has anybody tried to kill it?" said Jack.

"Can't kill it," said Vernon. "No man alive could kill a thing like this monster. Why it knocks whole trees over, pulls 'em out by the roots, grinds 'em into sawdust on the spot. It eats land two acres a mouthful, spits out boulders like peach seeds. It's eat a swath half-a-mile wide from here to Perry County already, ain't no man can kill a monster like that."

Jack grabbed his hoe and set out down the hill and Will and Tom followed along behind.

When they got to the road the boys saw neighbor Finley and his family walking along with big sacks of stuff on their backs. Finley's wife had a sack of clothes in one arm and her month-old baby in the other. The daughters were carrying quilts and blankets and the boys were carrying food and some pots and pans. Finley himself was carrying a ham under one arm and a crosscut saw over the other shoulder.

"Where you going with all that stuff?" said Jack.

"Ain't you heard about the monster?" said Finley. "They's the biggest old awful monster that ever was, running loose, eating up the world, and it's coming this way fast."

"Is anybody fighting it?" asked Jack.

"Fight it?" said Finley. "You get a look at that thing and you'll think otherwise. That monster get hold of you boys, he'll swallow you all down like three sardines."

Finley shifted his crosscut saw to the other shoulder and went on walking down the road.

"Well, at least tell us where it's at," Jack called after him.

"Just keep on the way you're going," Finley yelled over his shoulder. "You won't have no trouble finding that monster."

And the boys didn't, either. Before they'd gone another mile they commenced to hear the monster snorting and roaring and crashing around up on the hillside. Before long they could see its smoke-breath rising in the air. As the boys started up the hill, suddenly Tom yelled, "Look out boys, it's throwing rocks!" and they all dodged just in time to keep from getting run over by a big boulder.

"Over here!" Will yelled, waving his arms. He was standing underneath a rock ledge big enough for all three boys to hide under. Looking out, they could see the monster lurching and leaping and growling and roaring. It was the evilest-looking thing the boys had ever seen or heard tell of. It had a snout on the front that would reach out and wave around and then reach down and bite a chunk of ground big as a dwelling house. In front of the monster it was all trees and laurel and pretty ferns, and wet moss everywhere. But stretching out behind the monster, as far as their eyes could see, it wasn't anything but yellow mud and broken rocks.

"Lordy," said Will. "The end of the world has come."

"It'll be the end of us if we try to fight that thing," said Tom. "Let's give this up and go on home to supper."

"Ain't going to have no home if we don't stop this monster," said Jack.

"If we had some dynamite we might could blow one of its legs off," said Will.

"Could," said Jack. "But we don't want to blow up that man inside. We'll have to rescue him before we go to dynamiting."

"Poor feller," said Tom. "Watch at him, waving his arms around, helpless. I'm glad that ain't me in there."

"It'll be you if that monster gets hold of you," said Will.

"Boys, here's what to do," said Jack. "Will, you run back down to the road and tell the people coming by that we've got this monster cornered up here, and for 'em to come and help us fight it."

Without a word, Will crawled out from under the cliff and headed off downhill toward the road.

"Tom, you run out in front of that monster and dance around and wave your arms and cut a big shine, get its attention. I'm going to climb up the monster's side to where that man is and get him out."

"Run out there?" said Tom.

"Yes," said Jack. "Jump around, make it see you."

Tom's knees trembled at the thought. There was no way he could do something like that, but then, somehow, Tom did it anyway.

145

Well, as you might expect, when that monster seen Tom dancing around, it like to went crazy. It roared like thunder and struck out at him with its snout. But Tom jumped back out of the way and kept on waving his arms and jumping around. Once he faced the monster, he wasn't as scared as he thought he'd be.

"You old heathern," he yelled. "I ain't afraid of you."

When the monster struck at Tom again, Jack run out of the trees and leaped on the monster's side and started climbing up. Its hide was solid steel and there weren't many places to grab hold of. But Jack still had his hoe with him, and he was a good climber. By sticking the blade of the hoe in the little cracks in the monster's side and pulling himself up by the handle, it didn't take him long to get up to the monster's head where the captured man was.

"Come on!" Jack yelled at the man. "Break out of there and we can get away."

But somehow the prisoner couldn't hear Jack. The prisoner didn't notice Jack at all. It was like he'd been put under a spell. He just sat in there moving his arms around, looking straight ahead to the front where Tom was, and nothing Jack could do would get his attention.

Even after Jack hauled off and hit the monster's glass eye with his hoe and broke it all to pieces, still yet the prisoner didn't notice Jack. Jack started to grab him by the arm and just pull him out, but just as he reached in to do that, the monster caught Tom in its snout!

Jack could see Tom dangling out there plain as day as the monster lifted him high to eat him. Jack knew he didn't have any more time to fool around with the prisoner. He hated to hurt him but there wasn't anything else he could do. Jack hit the prisoner in the head with his hoe handle and knocked him to the floor inside the monster's head.

Soon as Jack did that, the strangest thing in the world happened. All of a sudden the monster quit its lurching and leaping and hushed its awful roar. Its big snout stopped in midair with Tom dangling down from it. The woods around fell quiet enough to hear a bird sing, and for a minute Jack couldn't believe it. He thought it was some kind of monster trick, to catch him in a lure.

Jack watched as Tom worked himself loose from the monster's grip and crawled up the length of the snout to the monster's head where Jack stood over the prisoner, who was still knocked out on the floor.

"We did it!" Tom shouted. "We killed the monster!" From his high perch he commenced to sing out across the trees to all the world. "The monster's dead! The monster's dead! Me and Jack killed the monster, and the awful old monster's dead."

Jack didn't feel like Tom did about it. He was glad the monster was dead and they'd all come through alive. But he didn't understand how knocking that poor prisoner out could stop the beast in its tracks. Jack didn't say anything about it to Tom. It was something he'd have to study on.

By the time Tom and Jack got back down to the ground with the prisoner, Will was back with a big crowd of people who'd come to fight the monster. By sundown that day there must have been a hundred people on the hill, looking at the dead monster and the strange man that had been a prisoner in its head.

The prisoner was almost as big a curiosity as the monster was. Being captured that way had addled him and caused him to talk crazy. When he first came to, he tried to fight Jack and Will and Tom.

"That monster's drove this poor man crazy," said Vernon.

"He's flew off in his mind," said Will.

"He'll be okay," said Mrs. Finley. "He just needs to rest up and be back among folks for awhile. We'll take him home and feed him a good supper, he'll feel better after that."

Some of the people around wanted to go ahead and blow up the monster, just out of revenge for all the damage it had done. But Jack said, "Why don't we just leave it here and let it rot? Let it lay here so people can come and see what it was they were so scared of. If another monster ever comes, maybe we won't be so scared next time."

So the people did that. They left the monster there to decay and sink into the ground. It wasn't long 'til it fell over on its side. It's still laying up there. You can go see it if you want to.

Jack Gets the Big-Head

ONE TIME a big monster came into Jack's district, eating up the land and scaring people away from their homes. Then Jack and his brothers Will and Tom went out and killed it.

You've probably heard that story.

But did you hear what happened to Jack after that? About him getting the big-head so bad he wouldn't hardly speak to people anymore?

Now the thing about Jack was that even before he killed that monster, he was well known around the mountains. He was a good hard worker, Jack was. He could do about any kind of farm work there was to do. And he was good-hearted, too. He was always ready to do favors for people, help them out when they needed it. Everybody that knew Jack liked him just an awful lot.

But then he went and killed that monster and got the big-head and Jack's friends didn't know what to think about him anymore.

Jack even got to acting proud around his brothers Will and Tom. He seemed to forget that they'd helped him kill the monster. Jack acted like he'd killed it by himself and on top of that, he acted like being a hero made him too good to do any work around the homeplace. Instead of going to the field with his brothers of a morning, Jack got so he'd sleep late, and when he would get up, he'd head out of the holler toward town, looking for people to brag to about killing the monster.

One day while he was in town standing around with a bunch of men swapping knives, a newspaper reporter came up and asked him if he was the same Jack that had killed the monster with a hoe-handle. Jack straightened up his shoulders, smoothed down his hair and said, "None other."

"Wait right here," said the reporter. And he ran into the hardware store and came back out with a hoe. He stuck the hoe in Jack's hand, then stepped back and took his picture. The next day that picture was in every newspaper in the land. "Jack The Monster-Killer," it said underneath. "Boy Kills Beast With Hoe."

Jack bought every newspaper he could find, then went around the district giving them away to people.

Will and Tom thought it was bad enough for Jack to be going around the district showing off so bad. But when they heard he'd been invited by the King to come to the capitol to receive the King's Award, the brothers knew that Jack was in bad trouble, and that they had to do something quick to help him.

"I can't think of nothing to do," said Will.

"Aunt Haze will help us," said Tom. And so the evening before Jack's train left for the capitol, Will and Tom finished up their chores and set out across the mountains to Ancient Creek to talk to old Aunt Haze about the problem.

They had to walk many hours to get to Ancient Creek and it was way past dark when they got to Aunt Haze's cabin. At first they thought there wasn't anybody home, but then, through a window, the boys saw a lamp burning inside and smoke coming out of the chimney, so they knocked on her door and Aunt Haze let the boys in.

Aunt Haze was glad to see Will and Tom. She didn't get much company anymore. In the old days, people used to come to her cabin to get her to doctor their wounds and ailments. Aunt Haze was a granny-woman, a midwife and herb doctor and, according to some, a witch who had supernatural powers. After the railroad came to the mountains and brought in modern times, people quit going to see Aunt Haze. Some were even afraid of her. They told scary tales about her having the evil eye and such.

But Will and Tom weren't afraid. They'd been brought up to love Aunt Haze and to trust her. Way back in the generations, Aunt Haze's people and their own were related, and Will and Tom were proud to claim kin to her. They looked on her as they would their real aunt, and every time anybody in Will's and Tom's family got sick or had troubles of any kind, they went to Aunt Haze for help.

As the boys sat on the bench in Haze's cabin, drinking sassafras tea and warming themselves in front of the fire, they told her what had happened to Jack. They told her about the big fight with the monster and how Jack had got so conceited over killing it they couldn't nobody stand to be around him anymore.

"Jack ain't struck a lick of work in a month," said Will.

"Me and Will has to do it all," said Tom. "We miss Jack helping us, but when we try to talk to him about it, he won't pay us no mind."

"All he wants to talk about is how he killed the monster," said Will. "He don't even remember that me and Tom helped him fight the thing."

"And now he's getting ready to go to the capitol, to accept the King's Award," said Tom.

Aunt Haze sat a long time, smoking her pipe and gazing at the fire in the grate. Finally she said, "Well, it's clear. Jack's been put under a spell and we've got to figure out a way to break it."

"A spell!" said Will.

"Oh Lord," said Tom. "They've got poor Jack under a spell."

"I've seen it on people before," said Aunt Haze. "It's a hard thing to cure. But it can be done if we do things right and do 'em quick enough. When's Jack's train leaving?"

"Sunrise tomorrow," said Tom. "He's spending tonight in the hotel over in town."

Aunt Haze leaned over to the fire and knocked the ashes out of her pipe. "That don't give us much time." She stood up then and went to the corner to get her shawl and her walking stick.

"Where you going?" asked Will.

"Don't slow me down with questions," Aunt Haze answered. "We've got a week's worth of walking to do in a single night, we can't waste no time. You all come on."

Will and Tom looked at one another, then at Aunt Haze. "We're tired out from getting here," said Tom. "We couldn't walk a night's worth in a night, let alone a whole week's."

"You can do a whole lot more than you think you can when you have to," said Haze. "But you can't do it sitting down. Come on now, time's a wasting."

Will and Tom weren't eager but they got up and followed Aunt Haze into the night. The moon was behind a thick cloud bank and it was dark as pitch in the woods. Before they'd gone ten yards along the path Tom tripped over a root and fell down, and Will fell down on top of him.

"It's too dark to walk," said Will.

Tom said, "I can't see a thing."

Aunt Haze told the boys to wait where they were. Then she stepped off the path into the trees and rummaged around behind an old half-rotten log. When she came back she was carrying a piece of bark covered with foxfire that shined like silver in the night. She broke the bark in two and then tied the pieces to her shoes with strands of wool she pulled out of her shawl. "Watch my feet," she said. "Put your feet where I put mine and you can walk forever and not get tired."

Will and Tom couldn't see anything except the foxfire on Haze's feet, but that was enough. They put their feet right where she put hers and followed Aunt Haze along the path through the dark woods.

Even though they couldn't see where they were going, the boys could tell they were going uphill. They felt the winding path rise up and up. As they got higher on the mountain they felt the air grow thin and cold. Just as Aunt Haze predicted, neither Will nor Tom got tired. But as the cold air cut through their skin and chilled their bones, they started complaining 'til finally Will said, "I can't go no further, Aunt Haze. It's too cold."

"I'm freezing to death," said Tom. And the brothers stopped on the trail and stood there shivering in the dark.

Aunt Haze didn't say a word this time. She just pulled two more strands of wool out of her shawl and tied one each around the boys' necks. Aunt Haze's great-great-great-great grandmother had made the shawl by hand, so far back in the ages even Haze didn't know just how old it was. The wool was of such quality that a single thread could keep a person warm, as Will and Tom learned when Haze tied the strings around their necks. Aunt Haze set out up the trail once more and Will and Tom followed on behind.

They were way up in the cliffs now. It was still nighttime, but it wasn't as dark among the cliffs as it was down in the trees. In the east the faintest trace of dawn was trying to light the sky. It wouldn't be long 'til sunrise. It would feel good to be in the sun again. But sunrise also meant that Jack's train would be leaving the depot over in town. Will and Tom hated to doubt Aunt Haze's wisdom, but here it was nearly sunrise, and as far as the boys could tell, she hadn't done a thing yet to help poor Jack. All she'd done was lead them out on an old mountain, so far away from town they'd never get back in time to save Jack. The boys were on the verge of telling Haze they didn't want to go any further when she stopped and announced that they'd reached their destination.

"But this ain't nothing but an old hillside," said Will.

"How come you to bring us way up here?" said Tom.

"This is where the Great Blue Eagle lives," said Aunt Haze. "He's going to help us do a week's worth of walking in a night."

As soon as Aunt Haze said that, a giant bird flew down from a crag and lit on a rock right next to where Will and Tom were standing. It was the biggest, fiercest-looking bird the boys had ever seen. If Will and Tom hadn't got their feet tangled up and fallen on top of each other in a heap, they'd have taken off running down that mountain fast as they could go.

Aunt Haze laughed as she picked the boys up and dusted off their clothes. "You boys are a sight," she said. "You don't have to be afraid of the Blue Eagle. He's our friend. He's going to help us break the spell they've put on Jack, and set him free. Ain't that right, Brother Eagle?"

"I'll help out any way I can, Aunt Haze," said the Blue Eagle.

Again Will and Tom tried to take off running when they heard the Blue Eagle talk. But Aunt Haze had hold of their shirttails and she made them stand there while she spent the next few minutes telling the Eagle about Jack's situation.

"What do you want me to do?" the Blue Eagle asked when Haze had finished talking.

"I want you to fly us on your back to every house in the district so we can tell the people that the reason Jack's been acting strange is because he's under a spell. The King's trying to trick Jack into coming to the capitol to work for him instead of staying home in the mountains and being with us. We need to tell the people that Jack's a prisoner on a train about to go away forever, and if we don't stop it none of us'll ever see Jack again. We've got to tell the people to get to the depot quick and not let that train leave 'til we rescue Jack out of it."

"That's easy enough," said the Blue Eagle. He flapped his huge wings and jumped down to the ground so Aunt Haze and the boys could climb onto his back.

"Oh Lordy, Aunt Haze, you don't mean we're going to fly on this Eagle," said Tom.

Will said, "I declare, I'd just as soon walk."

"Hush up and climb on here," Aunt Haze snapped as she settled herself on the Great Blue Eagle's back. "We ain't got time for foolishness."

Will and Tom weren't eager but they climbed on and held tight to Aunt Haze. With a great surge of his body and a powerful flap of his wings, the Blue Eagle soared into the air and flew out over the valleys of the district.

They flew in a circular pattern, going to the outlying houses first to tell the people to get to the depot quick, to stop the train. They landed at Garfield Quinn's house, then flew on to Miss Della Stack's homeplace at the head of Briar Branch. From house to house they went, giving the alarm.

The sun ball was above the horizon now, the sky was filled with light. As Will and Tom and Aunt Haze and the Blue Eagle continued on their circuit, they saw the roads in the valleys below filling up with wagons and horses and cars and pickup trucks, and hundreds of people heading for the railroad depot over in town. Aunt Haze told the Eagle to make one more circle around the district to make sure they hadn't missed anybody. When they'd done that the Eagle banked and turned then flew in a straight line toward town. The Eagle swooped down and lit on the roof of the depot.

"Look at all the people!" Will shouted as he and Tom and Aunt Haze climbed down.

"I've never seen such a crowd!" said Tom.

The driver of the train had never seen such a crowd either, especially one spread all over his railroad tracks. "You all get out of the way!" he shouted from his cab up in the engine. "This train's leaving for the capitol right away."

"Not 'til we rescue Jack, it ain't!" said someone in the crowd.

"Where's Jack at?" Will asked.

"Here he is!" said Arnold Fields. "In the first-class passenger car!"

Will and Tom and Aunt Haze ran back to the first-class car and sure enough, there was Jack, dressed like a Philadelphia lawyer, sitting in a seat all by himself, looking at his picture in the paper.

"Jack! Jack!" yelled Tom.

"Come on out, Jack. We've come to rescue you," said Will.

But Jack couldn't hear his brothers. He didn't appear to notice all the people standing around outside. Even when they all yelled, "Jack! Jack!" he still didn't pay any attention to them.

Suddenly the Blue Eagle flew down off the depot roof. With one quick peck of his beak the Eagle smashed the window of the railroad car. With his talons he reached in and snatched Jack by the coat collar, and before anybody in the crowd could say a word the Eagle flew off into the sky with Jack dangling.

They flew so high they nearly went out of sight. Then they came into view again as the Blue Eagle dived like a bullet straight down to the river. The Eagle dunked Jack good, then flew up high again. This time they didn't go out of sight. They flew in a circle above the people gathered on the ground.

"Jack, are you awake yet?" the Blue Eagle asked.

"I think I am," said Jack. "Unless this is all just a dream."

"It ain't no dream," said the Eagle. "You've been in a dream. But you're waking up now. Do you see all the people down there?"

"I see 'em," said Jack. "Who are they?"

"They're your friends and neighbors. They stopped the train to keep you from getting carried off to the capitol."

"The capitol?" said Jack.

"Yeah," said the Eagle. "You was about to ride the train to the city to accept the King's Award."

"What was I going to do that for?" asked Jack.

"You was under a spell," said the Eagle. "But you're waking up now. In fact, I think it's about time to drop you."

"Drop me!" Jack exclaimed.

"Yeah. But don't worry. The folks on the ground'll catch you. Are you ready to get back down to earth?"

"I reckon so," said Jack.

"Okay," said the Eagle. "Here you go." With a final flap of his wings to gain more altitude, the Blue Eagle opened his talons and down Jack went fast as a rock.

Before Jack could draw a breath, he was in the arms of his friends and neighbors. When they were sure they had a good grip on him, they stood Jack on his feet.

Henry Bentley said, "Well, Jack, how do you feel?"

"I feel grateful to you all for catching me," said Jack.

"We're glad to have you back among us," said Mrs. Spencer. "You've been gone a long time."

"Hello brother," said Will. And Tom said, "Hello Jack."

The brothers hugged each other. Then everybody started shaking hands.

"Where's Aunt Haze?" said Will. "Let her through so she can give Jack a hug, too."

The people looked around for Aunt Haze.

"We've got to find Aunt Haze," said Will. "If it wasn't for her, Jack would have been a goner."

"There she is!" someone in the crowd called out. "Up there!"

All the people looked into the sky. There was Aunt Haze, riding on the back of the Great Blue Eagle, heading for the distant hills. As the people watched, Aunt Haze stood up on the Blue Eagle's back and waved with both arms. The people waved back, and kept on waving as long as they could see her. Gradually she and the Eagle got smaller in the sky, and soon they disappeared.

"I owe a lot to Aunt Haze," said Jack as he watched her go.

"We all owe Aunt Haze a lot," said Will.

And Tom said, "We mustn't never forget her."

The people were turning away now to head home and get on with the new day's work. As Jack walked along between Will and Tom he said, "Boys, what kind of work are we doing today?"

"We're clearing out a new ground," said Tom.

"Getting it ready to plant," said Will. "Are you ready for a little work?"

"I'm ready," said Jack.

And the brothers walked on home together, arm in arm.

Balsam Morning

WHILE I WAS detoxing in Bluegrass Clinic my buddies Lee and Dexter and Paul and Rusty had gone on with their rowdy behavior as far as weekend drinking was concerned. We had all known for years that eventually we'd have to give up our weekend parties. It wasn't that we weren't intelligent and at least moderately educated drinkers. Twenty years ago Lee had gone to law school for two years before dropping out to help his father operate a radio station. "I'm two-thirds of a lawyer," he told people. After seven years in the Air Force Paul had become a paramedic and owner of an ambulance service in Finley County. Before his divorce and resulting obligation to pay his ex-wife serious alimony payments, Rusty had his own construction company. At one time Rusty hired Dexter as a drywall hanger. After the divorce they were both unemployed for several years. I was the editor of the local newspaper and the oldest one at fifty-three. When I came home from Bluegrass Clinic, after two weeks of proper diet, daily exercise and guided introspection, looking younger and healthier than any of them, it was instantly agreed that the time had come to give up all bad habits in preparation for the later stages of life.

I said I'd be glad to go camping but that I didn't plan on doing any drinking. They thought they'd try staying sober for a weekend themselves. Clearly the moment had arrived for us to actually do a thing we had talked about for years but had never managed. It was time for us to graduate from our adolescent behavior and quit drinking. But of course such momentous changes could not be brought about without certain solemn rituals and ceremonies. We decided to lay out on Balsam Ridge all night one more time.

The Friday night before our trip we partied pretty hard at Lee and Barbara's and so it went without saying that we weren't exactly efficient and well-organized outdoorsmen on Saturday morning. It was like wading through molasses trying to get ready to go camping. It took us all morning to load the quilts and tarps and coats and sweaters and skillet and coffee pot and jugs of water and a big ice chest full of beer and various other camping paraphernalia into Dexter's Buick station wagon. Barbara was amused by us would-be outdoorsmen but about noon she took pity on us and fixed us a sausage and eggs and gravy and biscuits breakfast.

It was two in the afternoon before we were ready to go. When we were all in the car and the motor was running, Barbara came over and leaned through the window to give Lee a goodbye kiss. Then, addressing the rest of us, she said, "It ain't like I want you all out of the house or nothing."

"We know that, Barbara," several of us said together.

"I mean, I really have no desire to just be quiet at home and watch TV and read magazines all weekend."

"But you're willing to sacrifice for us," said Dexter behind the steering wheel.

"I really would like to hear all the interesting things you say when you're drunk, especially since I haven't heard it since last night."

"This is our last party," Lee said sheepishly. "We're gonna be different men when we come back."

"I know you are," said Barbara. "Wilgus, you make sure Lee comes back a different person, okay?"

"I'll do it," I said. "It's at the very top of my agenda."

The breakfast gave us enough strength to drive to the County Line to get a fresh load of booze. We got to the liquor store and made our purchases easily enough but at the last minute Paul decided he had to run next door to the One-Stop Market to get some bread and baloney and Honeybuns to eat during the night, which made Dexter think of all the stuff he thought he ought to go buy, too.

When we were all loaded in the car again, ready to take off, Dexter decided he had to run back in the One-Stop and get some aspirins and a bottle of Nyquil to taper off on later that night. Then he wound up opening the bottle and spilling about a thousand aspirins on the floor before he'd even paid for them. Lee and me went in to help him pick his aspirins up, during which time a blonde woman that Rusty seemed to know pulled up to the gas pumps and he got into a private talk with her that took about twenty minutes to finish. As we all managed to get settled in the car again, Uncle Delmer walked up saying if he didn't get to the flea market over at Champion in half an hour his ex-wife Pauline wouldn't let him use her T-shirt booth to sell the do-dads he'd made during his recent time in the Veterans Hospital. I loved Delmer but this was too much for me. I leaned across Dexter who was in the driver's seat and stuck my head out the window and told Delmer that we were trying to get to Balsam Ridge before dark and we didn't have time to take him to Champion.

"Aw, hell, Wilgus," Paul yelled from the back seat. "We can give Delmer a ride."

"Why, yes," said Lee. "Climb in here, Delmer."

What this meant was twelve more miles in the wrong direction in addition to the fifteen miles out of the way we'd already driven to

161

get our liquor. I had to sit in the middle of the front seat so Delmer could have room for the sack of goods he was carrying.

"Delmer, you're not in the best of company, I reckon you know that," said Paul.

"I know," said Delmer. "I know you boys and your daddies, too." He grinned at me. "I especially know this one here."

"How you doing today, Delmer?" I asked him. I didn't want us to drive Delmer anywhere but I was glad to see him. Delmer had been one of my great friends all my life. He was the best guy in the world when he wasn't crazy or drunk or otherwise flew off in his mind.

"I'm doing very well," Delmer said. "Long as I get these goods over to Pauline. I'm sorry to interrupt you boys' trip."

"It don't matter," said Dexter. "We're on our way to Balsam to get drunk. Why don't you come lay out with us?"

Delmer looked around the car. He had about a four-day beard and his old clothes had their usual mildew smell. In his early life Delmer had been a dashing figure when he wasn't being a derelict. Somewhere along the way he had stopped being either dashing or a derelict and had learned to just be Delmer, an old man with peculiar ways that the local community made a place for. Today he looked bright-eyed and happy.

"Fifteen-year-ago next April I'd of been right with you boys," Delmer said.

"It's good to see somebody sober, Delmer," said Lee. "What have you got in your sack?"

"One thing and another," said Delmer. He opened his burlap sack and started taking things out and passing them around. He had stomach ulcers that put him in the VA hospital once or twice a year. He always came home with things he'd made in the craft shop. He usually made wallets and wrist bands and stuff out of leather but this time he'd whittled a bunch of crosses out of cedar, all about the size of your hand. There was one he'd made out of black walnut that he had shined to a high finish. He'd made several butterflies, too, by winding gold thread around nails he'd driven into boards in the shape of a butterfly.

"Why Delmer, these things are beautiful," I said. "How much are you going to sell these for?"

"I need six dollars apiece for my butterflies," he said. "My crosses is three dollars apiece, except that one there." He pointed to the shiny black walnut cross. "That one's for Pauline. She's started back to church here lately, I thought she might like something like that."

"If I had six dollars I'd buy this butterfly myself," said Paul. "Me 'n' my wife's been on the outs here lately, this butterfly might sweeten her up a little."

"What he means, Delmer, is that Rosette kicked him out for being a drug addict," said Wilgus.

"Well, she'd like this butterfly," said Delmer. "You can pay me later if you want to."

"That's a deal!" said Paul, and he reached across the car to shake Delmer's hand.

By the time we got to Champion we'd all bought crosses from Delmer on credit, and Paul and Lee had bought a butterfly apiece. We'd run through several more beers by the time we let Delmer out.

"You boys be careful," he said.

"We'll pay you your money, Delmer, don't you worry," Paul yelled to him out the window.

"I ain't worried," Delmer called back. "Everything's in the Lord's hands."

"Tell Pauline I'll see her this weekend," I yelled.

"I'll tell her," Delmer called back. "You boys come to Trace Fork Sunday, you'd all be welcome."

"Let's all get out and go to the flea market," Paul said. But Dexter was already steering the car onto the highway, headed back toward Whitaker and Route 15. An hour later we were at the mouth of Bonnet Creek on the far side of the county, starting up Balsam Ridge.

Balsam Ridge

IT WAS so rough driving up the Bonnet Creek road Dexter's Buick lost its muffler on a hairpin turn when both right-side wheels fell into a rain-washed gully. Instead of stopping to check the damage Dexter gunned the motor hard until the big car spurted forward in a deafening roar. Half a mile further on, near the top of Balsam Ridge, he jerked the steering wheel hard to the left, sending his vehicle off onto a faint overgrown trail. Dexter rammed the car through the briars and high weeds to emerge a moment later on an old strip mine that ran around the hill ahead of them like an abandoned road.

Dexter drove a hundred yards along the strip bench before he stopped. Thirty or so yards to the right rose the highwall from the mining. The sun had dropped behind the ridge by now and the air was turning chilly, so the men set directly to work establishing their camp for the night. From the back of the station wagon Lee and Paul hauled a heavy tarpaulin and spread it on the ground. Dexter gave himself the task of arranging rocks and slabs of shale in a circle for a fireplace, twenty yards out from the base of the strip-mine highwall. There was no shortage of rocks. They lay in profusion in a ragged row beneath the cliff where they had fallen over the years since Balsam Ridge had been stripped.

As Wilgus helped Dexter carry rocks to the fireplace, they heard Paul yelling from a ways on down the bench, "Hey guys, look at this!" They found him standing on a piece of corrugated roofing metal about ten feet long and three feet wide. The metal was bound to the ground by a thatch of vines and it took all their effort to pull it loose. They helped Paul carry the metal sheet to the camp where they placed it along one edge of the tarp, anchoring it in place with the ice chest full of beer.

Lee and Dexter carried the bags of groceries to the tin table on the ground. Paul assumed the duty of emptying the bags and arranging the contents in an orderly fashion. Around a thick roll of baloney, which he placed in the center, he set a rectangular box of government cheese, two loaves of light bread, chips and dips, mustard and mayonnaise, Fig Newtons and Moon Pies, packets of Honey Buns, jars of pickles and pickled pigs' feet, cans of sardines and viennie sausages, a large box of saltine crackers, jars of peanut butter and jelly, chocolate syrup and marshmallow cream.

"All the major food groups," Paul said.

Meanwhile, Wilgus and Rusty set out walking along the strip bench to look for firewood. The original woods that once had lined the sides of Balsam Ridge had been scraped away by the mining but there was no shortage of old timbers and posts and boards scattered along the bench. They began carrying four-by-fours of varying lengths and several sheets of half-rotted weather-boarding to the camp and dumping it in a pile. Next to the wood Lee had started a coal pile, scooping small pieces of coal from the ground with a rusted hubcap he had found.

By eight p.m. the campers were putting the finishing touches on their domestic accommodations. By nine p.m. full dark had come and the men had arranged themselves in a half circle around the fire. Wilgus sat cross-legged in the dirt next to the ice chest, turning the dial of Dexter's Sanyo blaster. He was searching for the

Hazard radio station that played Big Band music every Saturday evening from seven until ten. Unable to get anything on the radio but static, he flipped to the CD player and put in his Stagedoor Canteen music from the war years. He had intended to save this album for later in the evening, even as he also was holding back a secret pint of Scotch and a three-pound ham in a can for the midnight hour of the party.

As a seasoned veteran of many drunken evenings with this particular crew, Wilgus knew well the need for keeping back a few trump cards. To manage to be the drunkest, yet still best functioning, most intact and inspired one in the later hours of the party was an art they all aspired to perfect. But after years of practice, only Wilgus had ever managed to get truly good at it. His stashes might include secret assets such as flashlight batteries, tape cassettes, bottles of superior liquor, or hidden gourmet foods. Such items were vital resources with which to gain control over one's pals as they became progressively too impaired to defend themselves from the manipulations of the most sober one, come midnight.

"Wilgus, Lee said you've been in the nuthouse in Lexington," said Dexter. "Is that true?"

"I didn't say it was a nuthouse," Lee protested. "I said he was in the asylum."

"Was it like jail?" asked Paul. "Did the judge send you there?"

Wilgus sipped his beer and stared into the fire. "It was kind of a nuthouse. They call it a clinic, Bluegrass Clinic. You could say it's like an asylum, a place of rest. You can rest pretty good there."

"Where is this place?" Paul asked. "I might need to check in myself sometime."

"Out from Lexington," said Wilgus. "You volunteer to go there. My shrink recommended it."

"You got a shrink?" asked Paul.

"Of course he's got a shrink!" Dexter hissed at Paul in comic umbrage. "Do you think that at Wilgus's precarious time of life he would be shrinkless?"

"I would never think Wilgus was shrinkless," said Rusty.

"Not for one minute did I think he was shrinkless," said Lee, shaking his head. "Jesus, Paul. Just because you're shrinkless doesn't mean everybody else is."

"Well, how was I to know?" said Paul defensively. "I ain't seen Wilgus in a damn year!"

"My shrink's name is Helen," said Wilgus. "She thought I ought to check in for awhile so I did. It was strange but I wound up liking it pretty good. Dried out. Learned a lot. Quit drinking." Wilgus marked this last statement by holding up his beer and taking a drink.

Rusty said, "Boys, I hate to interrupt all this psychiatry but who wants to go out around the mountain with me?" He'd been working for a full minute to raise himself from his semi-prone position.

Understanding his comrade's poetic statement to be an invitation to step beyond the circle of firelight to take a manly piss, Wilgus said, "I'll go," and began his own effort to bring himself upright. The men walked to the edge of the strip bench and looked into the dark valley below. "Is that Dobb's Fork?" asked Wilgus.

"That's Watt's Branch," said Rusty. "Flows into Dobb's Fork."

"There was a good ball player from Dobb's Fork," said Wilgus. "Houston somebody."

"I remember him," said Rusty. "He could dribble with either hand."

"He played for Morehead for awhile I think," said Wilgus.

"One year," said Rusty. "I don't know where he wound up."

"He was a good player," said Wilgus. The men zipped their pants and headed back to the fire.

When Wilgus resumed his place among his fellows he surprised himself by opening his bottle of Scotch, taking a sip, replacing the cap, handing the bottle to Dexter and stretching out on the ground with his feet toward the fire.

"Looks like Wilgus has gone to bed," said Paul.

"Wilgus, don't quit on us," said Dexter. "It ain't even midnight yet."

"He's already dreaming," said Rusty.

"I wonder what about?" said Lee.

"Probably about that woman shrink he talks to," said Paul. "He's in love with her."

"Wilgus, you ain't dead, are you?" said Dexter, nudging Wilgus's foot with his own.

"He's only sleeping," said Paul.

"Waiting for Jesus to come," said Rusty.

Lee stood up and disappeared into the darkness and returned to the circle with a foot-square slab of shale. "Boys, if he's dead, it's only right that our friend Wilgus Collier have a proper burial," said Lee. He leaned down to place the shale on Wilgus's chest, which immediately inspired all the mourners to find their own shale slab to place on and around their reclining colleague. Paul laid a thin slab on Wilgus's stomach while Dexter and Rusty leaned two slabs together to form a spacious pyramid over his head.

Wilgus felt the slabs of stone against his legs, his chest, over his arms, against his feet. It felt oddly comforting. He thought, this shale, these rocks, a million years to form. These hills submerged by oceans, every coal seam a forest, drowned by the returning ocean to harden over yet more eons into another seam and then another. All the coal-rich mountains of the Cumberland Plateau receding, the forest returning in its own time, watersheds forming, Breaks of Sandy, Clover Fork, three forks of the Kentucky, each its own river combining to make the main channel, all part of the Ohio River Valley.

Wilgus could easily have pushed away the stones that covered him but spiritually he wasn't ready. Something else must happen, some event, some word or song or more prayers take place before he could free himself of the stones. Now was the time to simply lie on the cold clay of the strip bench in acceptance of everything as it was, all reality. Whiskey. Friends. Fire. Vast dark universe hovering above the fragile human scene on a strip-mined mountain in Finley County, Kentucky, USA, North America, planet Earth, surrounding all. He breathed quietly, listening to the sweet language of his buddies, taking in through his eyelids the yellow firelight that filtered through the gaps and spaces of the stones. *Breathe. Let the breathing breathe itself, no intention, take a break from all intention, breath and body know what to do, my father dead at thirty-eight, I am fifty-three, he'd be seventy-nine now if he had lived, fifty-three from seventy-nine equals twenty-six, Glen at twenty-six, me at twenty-six.*

Through the shale Wilgus sees the fire burn brighter as his buddies add wood to the flames. He watches Lee sprinkle a handful of coal dust he'd gathered from the base of the highwall earlier in the evening. Wilgus sees a swirl of images floating like dust motes on the air. He sees Main Street of Blaine, Christmas season, light snow falling, holiday lights blinking, drone of voices, throngs of people on the sidewalks, the sounds make a music in his mind that lingers even as the picture blinks away and Wilgus sees himself as a child at twilight time lying on a quilt in the backyard at the homeplace next to a circle of grownups lounging in lawn chairs, talking quietly among themselves, their voices a low tone. Grandma, Granddad, Evelyn, Junior, his father Glen. Wilgus feels the quilt's cool fabric in which the family story is recorded, he smells the new-mown grass with fresh dew on it, grass growing on the surface of the world. Above the world, stars are blinking on one by one as Wilgus breathes the night air of his vision.

All time has tended toward this moment, every act, every gesture in his fifty-three years has led him to this hour on this industrial mountain waste ground, union of forever and of now. *My dad was industrial waste. In World War I, General Haig referred to the English dead as "wastage." What's left of these hills and valleys and hollers and coves and bottomlands by the streams, all will wither and die, dry up and blow away with no trace. A thousand ages from now, the Appalachian mountain chain, Nova Scotia to North Georgia, returning to its place a thousand fathoms beneath the sea.*

"Ask Wilgus how's everything in the passed-out business," Lee said to Paul, who was sitting closest to the supine newspaperman.

"Wilgus, get up and piss, the world's on fire," said Dexter.

"Somebody preach," said Rusty. "Time to funeralize."

"Friends, let's bow our heads in prayer," Lee began. "Let's pray for our good friend Wilgus Collier here, lying in a sweet attitude of death."

"He was a good man," Paul intoned.

"And sorry and no count," Dexter added with perfect timing.

"At the same time!" put in Rusty.

"Wilgus was balanced in those ways," said Paul.

"But highly imbalanced in others!" Wilgus called out from the grave.

"He speaks!" said a shocked and horrified Dexter.

"Quick, roll away the stones," commanded Rusty.

"Touch not the stones!" Paul called out. "Leave him be."

"But he might need to scratch," said Lee.

"We need to pray some more, boys," said Paul. "Lord, as bad off as Wilgus is in some of his ways, he's worthy of heaven. He's done bad things, and he's done good things. Let's deal with the bad things first. I don't want to go into too many details but, briefly, Wilgus's main fault is that he keeps to hisself too much. Sometimes whole weeks'll go by and you can't get him to drink with you at all."

"Lord, sometimes Wilgus just stands around on Main Street, staring at the tops of the buildings," said Dexter. "He scares people."

"We know where he went wrong," Lee said. "It was when he run with the hippies out there in California."

"It started before that," said Paul. "It started when he got above his raising."

"And when was that?" Rusty inquired.

"When he went away to that school in Chicago."

"You all ain't prayin'!" Wilgus yelled. "You're just bullshitting!"

"We do need to be more respectful," said Paul. "If this ain't a semi-serious situation, I've never seen one."

"Lord, let me interrupt here," said Lee. "My colleagues are all sorry heatherns, and they're drunk. They're such bad sinners theirselves they can't even pray right. I can't sit here and let 'em lowrate a good man like Wilgus Collier. Forget what they said about him and let's start all over. Lord, we're gathered around this fire to pray for our good friend Wilgus Collier, who reposes in death right here beside us."

Wilgus dreamed on beneath his stones.

Epilogue

Author's Note

MANY YEARS AGO at Stanford University I had the good
fortune to study for six months with Irish short story writer Frank
O'Connor. In writing classes Mr. O'Connor spoke much about the
short story as a literary form, but personal stories about ordinary
life as told in casual conversation had a place in his concept as
well. I was only twenty-three in a seminar of far more sophisticated
writing students. My stories about growing up in a coal mining
family in Appalachia in the 1940s interested Mr. O'Connor. He
and I developed our own out-of-class conversation. Our subject
was our working-class family backgrounds, his in County Cork, my
own in the coalfields of eastern Kentucky. Mr. O'Connor was one
of the first articulate grownups I had met who knew how to hear
my stories about growing up in the Appalachian mountain region.
That such a literary figure would give me his personal attention
was a major source of encouragement for me as a young writer.

Sixty years later, I am still thinking about my early-life coal camp
experiences and hillside farm experiences among my mother's people
as well. All of the stories in *Allegiance* are based on personal memories.
Most are told by my fictional character Wilgus Collier. Wilgus and
I go back a long way. Originally Wilgus was a fictional character
in a series of short stories, some of them in my collection *Kinfolks*.
Now, for better or worse, here he is again in what I intended to

be autobiographical stories. Although the first section of *Allegiance* is autobiographical fiction, the epilogue features four stories that are straightforward autobiography, "Storied Ground," "Jerry," *"Look Homeward, Angel,"* and "Mr. Frost." But in the final story in the epilogue, a stream-of-consciousness piece called "Shattered Jewel," Wilgus reappears, along with Uncle Delmer and members of my fictional Collier family. As one perceptive reader of *Allegiance* observed, where Wilgus and Gurney are concerned, "the lines between selves blur."

I wanted to end this collection with a stream-of-consciousness story because it returns us to that place which has not been "worded" yet, a place of imagination and dream life and memory. The human mind is restless and curious. Anybody can feel that there is something just beyond what we know. And some of us want to know what that next thing is, or what that further realm of thought is. My Jungian therapist in California in the early 1970s might say we are venturing into the border regions of the psyche where human consciousness flows into cosmic consciousness. This feels very Appalachian to me. My starting place as a writer and my identity and my thinking is as a regionalist. But then you realize that the Appalachian region is infinite. If we think about landscape, about mountains, there's more than one valley. There are valleys off of valleys off of valleys, and finally they're called hollers. A holler or a cove is infinite in its own way.

In writing about myself, my life, my family history, I inevitably return to the subjects of place, region, landscape and watersheds where my family story has been enacted. In ways similar to the Kentucky River and its sources in eastern Kentucky, I can say that nearly all my creative work as writer, and film and television narrator, has its sources in the mountains of eastern Kentucky. Even after a hundred years of literary and media attention to those Kentucky mountain counties, they are still little known or understood by people who have not lived there.

Appalachia, with its distinctive story traditions, is the ground from which these stories come. The great thing about Appalachian literature is that even as it now includes all the traditional genres and some newly invented ones as well, it has not abandoned its folk roots. When Wilgus is in Bluegrass Clinic, suffering, dislocated, hallucinating, two Jack tales suddenly appear, which is a natural thing although it may not feel like it at first.

To heal, Wilgus needs to find, to recover, what scholars sometimes call "the Jack quality." Jack is smart, but he is also clever. Cleverness is a quality that the folk hero has. And the folk hero is not hostile to the idea of supernatural forces. Folk belief is different than intellectual belief. It is trust in the common people, trust in ordinary people. Jack is a connection to the hidden magic of daily life. Sometimes he is dumb, sometimes he gets in trouble, but then an unseen force will rescue him. Often, it is the community that sets him straight. Sometimes Jack does the rescuing.

The thing about Jack is he always lands on his feet. Jack is never defeated. He's wounded but he's never beaten. Jack has not been sanitized and processed and educated and trained for a bourgeois life. He is a connection to folk knowledge, a connection to competence, compassion, affection, and willingness to help one another. And finally, I think Jack is consistently a good-hearted, positive energy force in the community.

In my life and writing, I am out front as a regionalist. I think of *Allegiance* as a regional collection, intimate and neighborly. The book brings together a group of my writings that spans decades. To gather and arrange them here has been an occasion to consider the phenomenon of memory itself. Most people "have a head full" of personal memories. Families, communities, nations all have shared memories that help bind their members in a common story to which individual members may feel deep allegiance. Sometimes such feelings are so strong we must write them down. In this book, I write of my allegiances to places and people, to language and story making, to experiences that have stayed with me throughout my life, and allegiance to memory itself.

It is a pleasure to see the stories in a new conversation with each other on these pages, and in a new conversation with readers. I wish I could have given Mr. O'Connor a copy of *Allegiance*.

GURNEY NORMAN

Storied Ground

WHEN I WAS A KID in the 1940s and early 1950s my older brother and younger sister and I lived much of the time on a farm with our maternal grandparents in Lee County, Virginia, near the small railroad town of Pennington Gap. From time to time we also lived with our father's parents in a coal camp called Allais, near Hazard in Perry County, Kentucky. As a crow might fly, it's only about twenty air miles from Pennington Gap to Hazard. But on the narrow, winding, two-lane mountain roads that linked the two towns in those days, the driving distance was closer to ninety miles. Those roads crossed some of the most rugged and beautiful mountain country in the Appalachian coalfields, and some of the most storied ground in all of North America.

We kids lived with our grandparents because our parents had become casualties of life at early ages. At the height of World War II, in 1944, when I was seven, my mother was committed to a state mental hospital a few months after my father was drafted into the U.S. Army. By 1948 he himself was a patient at a Veterans Hospital suffering from diabetes and related illnesses. In the absence of our parents, my sister and brother and I came to regard our two sets of grandparents' houses as our two homes.

This was not a simple or easily managed arrangement. We were only eight and seven and five years old but all three of us children knew that between the parents of our parents, no love was lost. Each side tended to blame the other for what they perceived to be the ruination of our parents and our little nuclear family. We didn't understand the family politics in which we kids sometimes seemed like pawns, but the furious in-law arguments and disputes were on full display before our widely opened eyes. To be sure, we were much loved and doted upon by each set of relatives, very well-cared for in every respect. All these years later I remain filled with vast love for each and every one of my family members on each side. Most of them are buried in Appalachian ground and I visit their graves as often as I can. But it remains true that we children were allowed to see and hear adult behavior and talk that we had best been shielded from.

One time when I was five my mother and I were riding in her mother-in-law's car on the stretch of road between Allais and downtown Hazard. After a mile or so of short-tempered nagging, suddenly my grandmother stopped the car by the roadside and ordered my mother to get out. This sudden, almost violent escalation stunned my mother. She and my father owned no car. When they didn't walk or ride buses or taxis they depended on my grandmother to take them places. Now my mother was being set out on the road by her mother-in-law. I can never forget looking out the rear window of my grandmother's Buick at my mother standing alone beside the road, watching us drive away. The picture of her in that moment on that single, certain point on the landscape is indelibly printed in my memory and my feelings. Half a century later, every time I drive past this spot of ground, I still see my mother standing there and feel the emotions of that day all over again.

The story of that experience is inscribed upon the land.

Ten years later, the summer of 1952, my father got a furlough from the Veterans Hospital and came to Pennington Gap to visit my sister and me at our grandmother's house in Virginia. My mother was still in the mental hospital but Grandma was hospitable to her son-in-law. As the years had gone by and we kids had grown older by a decade, the old furor of the in-fighting among the relatives had eased. Grandma even brought out her last ham from the smokehouse to serve to my dad, and otherwise treated him well.

The morning my dad left to return to the hospital I walked with him down the hill to catch the bus. It was painful for him to walk more than a few yards at a time because his ankles were grossly swollen from the insulin injections he took for his diabetes at the hospital, so we left the house with plenty of time to spare. I offered to carry the cardboard box my dad used as a suitcase but he insisted on carrying it himself. Even walking slowly we got to the highway early. The usual place to wait for the bus was by the mailbox which my grandfather had mounted on a locust post beside the road some years before. But my dad's feet were hurting badly by this time so we looked around for a place to rest. A few yards behind us a narrow wooden bridge stood across Cane Creek which flowed sluggishly through a small weed-filled bottom sprinkled with willow trees. Carefully my father propped his cardboard box against the locust post, then walked with me to the bridge where we leaned against its railing in the shade of a willow tree.

My father and I had talked pretty relentlessly during his visit so in our interlude on the bridge neither of us felt a need to say much more. We looked down at the water and across the pleasant valley formed by Cane Creek. After awhile my father began to talk about his vision to someday gather our scattered family together again and build a house somewhere in the mountains, perhaps over near Hazard, or there in the Powell Valley, in Lee County. He had mentioned the idea in some of his letters but I had never paid much attention to it. But hearing him describe it in conversation was different and I listened as if hearing it for the first time. He said he'd be getting out of the hospital before long, and that my brother and sister and I were old enough now to help him make a nice home for our mother. I didn't need to believe in his vision to appreciate hearing him speak it so earnestly. I had never felt closer to my father than in those few minutes on the little bridge over Cane Creek.

When the bus finally came into view we started walking back toward the mailbox. My dad walked so slowly he waved me on ahead to flag the bus down. When the bus stopped and the door opened, my father hurried along the best he could while I retrieved his box to have it ready. Puffing from exertion, my father took the box with one hand and with the other squeezed my shoulder before pulling me to him in a one-armed hug. Then we shook hands. The driver waited until my father had found a seat before closing the door and easing the bus back onto the road.

My father died in the VA Hospital six months later so that was the last time I ever saw him alive. Nearly fifty years later, the bridge over Cane Creek still stands, as well as the place, the space, by the road where he boarded the bus. To this day I can't drive through that little valley without stopping to stand awhile and think about my dad and all the times when I was a child recording such scenes and feelings. When I visit Cane Creek, or any of the hundreds of other places in the mountains where I have similar attachments, I always come away refreshed. The visits are rituals I conduct for myself by which I revive memories and stories that are precious to me, and through which I remind myself that I am still a feeling creature, capable of love.

By the middle-1950s the new medicines had allowed my mother to leave the hospital and resume a more-or-less normal life, albeit in sheltered environments at her mother's home, and later with my sister and her family. In spite of years of shock treatments and confinement my mother had a remarkable capacity to recall the minute details of experience from decades before. In the last years of her life I used to take her on long drives through the mountains of eastern Kentucky and southwestern Virginia to visit places that she felt attached to from her early life there. Our road trips together were the best storytelling situations I have ever been part of, which is saying something because I have lived much of my life among the great storytellers of our times. Often as we drove past totally empty places along the roadside my mother would point and then tell me about the building that used to stand there and the people who had lived there or perhaps worked there in some long-defunct country store or filling station. After a few years of driving the old familiar routes we reached the point where I had heard most of the stories before. But it didn't matter. Stories are meant to be told and retold, again and again, not just by the original tellers but by others in a family or community who have recognized them as living treasures to be cared for and handed on.

One of the stories my mother told most often was about the first time she ever laid eyes on my father. It was the fall of 1928 on the campus of Lincoln Memorial University, a small college at Harrogate, Tennessee, only a mile from the famous Cumberland Gap through which the pioneers traveled en route to Kentucky. Cumberland Gap is a majestic feature on the landscape at the western end of Powell Valley forty miles west of Pennington Gap, so any time we found ourselves that close we always drove on to Harrogate to spend a few minutes on the LMU campus. We would only stay fifteen or twenty minutes, long enough for her to show me again the places on the campus grounds that still held power for her. She always showed me the dorm she had lived in, and the athletic fields where she had run the low-hurdles. And always she showed me where she had stood the first time she saw my father, a tall, dark haired young man ambling across a lawn that sloped down toward her dorm.

Someone introduced them that same day and it wasn't long at all before they went on a Sunday afternoon hike to the Gap together. After spending an afternoon scrambling along the trails that wound up the steep hillsides, they returned to the base of the mountain, to the small town named after the famous pass through the towering mountain above: Cumberland Gap. Not far from the railroad depot in the town was the southern entrance to a tunnel that ran beneath mighty Cumberland Mountain to connect the Powell River Valley of Virginia and Tennessee on the south side of the mountain with the headwaters of the Cumberland River of Kentucky on the north side. My parents, both eighteen-year-old college freshmen, walked all the way through the tunnel and back again before returning to campus.

You all didn't stop and have a little kiss in there, did you? I teased my mother the first time she told me this story. She looked at me grinning and said, yes.

Sometimes after one of our brief visits to the LMU campus I would drive us down the hill to Cumberland Gap town and park by the old railroad depot a hundred yards or so from the very same tunnel entrance my parents had walked through. The stonework that formed the arch was itself satisfying to look at, an enduring monument to the unknown workers whose hands had laid those stones. The dark portal seemed like the entry point to a realm of mysterious dimensions. My mother was content to sit in the car with the motor turned off and just look at the entrance but my urge to go inside the tunnel, to have my own relationship to it, was strong, and in time I started making my own solitary pilgrimages to Cumberland Gap's railroad tunnel. When I walked into the tunnel alone the first time the dark and the quiet appealed to me immensely. It felt deeply natural to me to be alone in a dark, moist world inside the earth. My father and grandfather and several uncles had all worked in the mines at one time or another so I'd been in coal mines many times. The cool air, the slate smell of cold wet stone, the lingering odor of old coal smoke from the days of the steam engines were familiar sensations. I carried a flashlight but didn't use it until, in the middle of the tunnel, I decided I wanted to get a look at the rivulet of water flowing beside the tracks. All the way in from the entrance I'd heard water trickling but it seemed to make a different sound at that mid-point in the tunnel and I wanted to see why that might be.

At first I couldn't believe my eyes but then there was no mistaking: from a little pool of swirling water no bigger than my two cupped hands, the stream divided and flowed in opposite directions! I shined my light on the water that ran back the way I had come. Then I shined it on the other stream bubbling toward the far end of the tunnel. Separate streams from a single source. Neither stream was more than three inches wide, but for a moment I felt as if the very Mississippi had somehow divided, as if the laws of nature had been repealed.

But after sitting and thinking in the dark for awhile the world no longer seemed divided. The certainty of nature and her processes settled around me again like a dark cloak. I knew that outside in the world of sunlight and moon and starry skies, rain falls on

185

Cumberland Mountain. Then it evaporates, soaks in or runs off either flank, south and north, obeying gravity. Deep underground, the water must also follow gravity. Far below the dividing ridge of Cumberland Mountain the water table divides, draining into separate watersheds, south and north, just as it has drained since the mountains themselves were formed untold millions of years ago.

As I sat there, listening to the water, I felt awed by it, awed by the mountain and its dark passageway, awed by time, by space, awed by the fact that my parents, young students on their first date, had once upon a time passed through the very underground space I now occupied. They were part of the human history of that mountain and now so was I. Perhaps here where the waters divided was where they had paused for their kiss. It pleased me very much to think so. It filled me with joy to be that close to my mother and father in that dark place, that kiva. In an uncanny way I felt that I had been there with them when they kissed, and that they were here with me now.

Jerry

PRETEND THAT I have presented a full account of my life up to age nine, and told the basic story of being sent at age four to live with my paternal grandparents in Allais coal camp near Hazard. My six-year-old brother and three-year-old sister still lived with our parents in a small frame house in Walkertown, half a mile away. It was never explained to me why the grownups made the decision to send me to live with my grandparents but, looking over the course of my long life, it was a momentous event, the first of many that marked my turbulent childhood.

Then came World War II. By 1944, the American war effort required that men well into their thirties, including our thirty-four-year-old father, be drafted. This meant that our mother, a vibrant elementary-school teacher, would move with us kids to her parents' hillside farm, a hundred miles of mountain roads distant in Lee County, Virginia. Our mother's parents, whom we kids knew as Grandma and Granddad, were wonderful, loving, competent people who had raised eight children of their own, our mother was their second child. They welcomed us little Kentuckians and we adapted to "country" life quickly, though the full story of this change for us all would require many pages of another book. For now let me just say that by the end of the next two years, our mother had developed mental illness and been committed to a state mental hospital, our father had returned from the Army, his health so deteriorated he was virtually unemployable. His father, for whom I am named, had suffered a health collapse at age sixty-five which ended his working life. This included his claim on the coal company house in which he and my grandmother had lived for twenty-five years and raised my father and his young brother Lucian who had died of tuberculosis in 1934 at age twenty-two.

What was to be done with the children as the 1946 school year approached, who would keep us, where would we go to school? The basic goodness of people supplied the answer. My young sister Gwynne, age seven by now, would live with Grandma and Grand-dad on their small hill farm in Virginia. My ten-year-old brother Jerry and I were sent to Clear Creek Baptist church camp in Knox County for two weeks in June while our Norman grandparents uprooted themselves from their comfortable Allais home.

School had already begun when my brother and I were at last settled for the school year at Stuart Robinson School. Settled for the next five years, actually, thanks to earnest Christian people who had taken it as their mission to serve and care for children where the need existed. Stuart Robinson School in mountainous Letcher County, Kentucky, had been founded by Presbyterians near Blackey in 1914 as soon as the railroad connected the area to the modern world.

By the time my brother and I were enrolled at Stuart Robinson in 1946 the modern twenty-acre campus featured six brick buildings: dormitories for girls and boys, a gymnasium, a library, a modern classroom building and a residential building for teachers. On its thirty-acre farm the school maintained its own dairy of sixteen cows which produced fresh milk and butter daily for a hundred boarding students, faculty and staff who lived on campus, and several hundred public "day" students in grades one through twelve. I feel that I owe my very life to this school. Except for summers, I lived there for nine years, from age nine in 1946 until I graduated at eighteen in 1955. I grew up on that campus. It shaped my life.

For five and a half of the nine years, my brother Jerry was a huge part of my experience at Stuart Robinson School. Jerry had been a "chubby" boy until he was twelve but by thirteen he was beginning to develop as a strong athletic young man, not just physically but emotionally and psychologically too. At fourteen, a high school freshman, he became a work-scholarship student and was placed in charge of the SRS campus central-heating system, in charge of the huge furnace beneath the library that heated every building on campus through a system of underground pipes. Coal was fed to the fire in the furnace from two stokers that needed to be kept full at all times in the cold winter months. This obliged Jerry to fill the stokers by hand, using a shovel, at five every morning, and to check them all day and night. It was a man's work. Jerry played fullback on the football team and he made good grades in his classes. At sixteen Jerry was very much a man.

In my freshman year of high school, fall of 1951, I joined Jerry on the football team. As a 135-pound newcomer I didn't play in any of the games but every day in season we practiced on the field in the center of our campus and we took our team scrimmages seriously. I often didn't even get in our team's practice games but sometimes the coach would have me play defensive end for a few plays near the end of practice. Jerry and his first-team buddies ran roughshod over us third-teamers. Gradually, though, I figured out a way to bring my big fullback brother down. I stopped trying to tackle him. Instead I waited until he had smashed through our line and as he passed by me I would get hold of the back of his belt, and as he dragged me down the field behind him I would grab one of his feet with my hand and down he would go. He always gained five or six yards in spite of my strategy, but it was a victory to keep him from getting ten or twelve.

After the 1951 football season, just a week before the end of the fall semester, Jerry left Stuart Robinson School and enrolled in Hazard High School. I have never understood his reasons. I do remember that one Friday night he and another dormitory boy left the campus without permission and went to the village of Isom eight miles away for hamburgers. It was unlike Jerry, a high-school sophomore, mature in so many respects, to behave so frivolously. He was missed by the housemother and the school principal became involved. In five years, this was the first time he had been in trouble with the school authorities. He returned to our room around 6:00 a.m. With no word of explanation, he threw a few clothes in a pillow case and walked off the campus and that quickly, I was alone in my dorm room.

Three and a half school years later, I was asleep in my room when our housemother Mrs. Breeding came in and said, Gurney, you need to wake up and I woke up. It was 2:30 in the morning, May 6, 1954. Julius, an ambulance driver for Engle Funeral Home in Hazard, was with Mrs. Breeding. I was told that my brother Jerry had been hurt in a car wreck in Hazard and I needed to go with Julius to the hospital. It was raining.

Jerry had always been good at getting summer jobs. In the summers after he left Stuart Robinson School, he had been a construction worker in northern Kentucky and could afford to have his own car. With three weeks remaining before his graduation, Jerry's car needed minor repairs and was in a mechanic's garage overnight. Ordinarily it would have been Jerry driving friends about town in the evening, perhaps to get a hamburger, perhaps just for the pleasure of cruising. But with his car in the shop he was out with his buddies in a car driven by a lawyer's son who had piled seven boys, counting himself, into his daddy's car and then driven so fast he lost control of the car which left the road, struck a ditch, bounced up the embankment and landed across the railroad tracks in front of an approaching coal train. The car doors were so damaged in the first part of the wreck they would not open so the boys struggled to exit through the windows. I later learned that Jerry, from his place in the middle of the back seat, was able to push some of the boys out the windows before the train smashed into the car and pushed it a hundred yards down the railroad tracks.

On our way to the hospital to see Jerry, Julius told me that at the scene of the wreck Jerry, though obviously hurt, had been able to get into the ambulance by himself and sit upright in the passenger seat, the seat where I was sitting now. He said Jerry spoke only once on the ride to the hospital. "I feel real bad," Jerry said. When they arrived at the hospital in Hazard, Jerry managed to walk to the door and enter the hospital on his own.

I don't remember my feelings as I entered the hospital through the same door hours later. I was met by two nurses, Benedictine nuns, who escorted me to the elevator and to the third-floor waiting room, where my grandmother, whom we kids called "Auntie," was seated on a couch crying. There wasn't much to say. There wasn't anything to say. A nurse led me down to the end of a hall where my brother lay on a stretcher under a sheet, his eyes closed, breathing normally or so it seemed. His clothes, which included a baseball player's jersey, were folded on a nearby chair. His dark hair was tousled but his expression seemed normal, not "serene" but relaxed. I was aware that he was unconscious, but his expression was familiar, my same brother. The nun left me and there I was with my big brother, apparently asleep.

I stayed with him until around 6:00 a.m. Then Auntie and I went to her apartment and slept three hours, at least I did. By 9:30 a.m. we were back at the hospital and I was beside Jerry again and it was strange: he lay exactly as he had lain before, in the hall, covered by the sheet, hair and expression the same, clothes in the same place, same arrangement. He was still lying on the stretcher at the end of the hall. There was no indication that he had been touched, or even seen, certainly not treated. There was no one standing by, no medical people coming or going. No tubes, no sign of attention. I never saw any medical person in the vicinity of Jerry while I was there. No doctor or nurse spoke to me during the night or that morning. It didn't occur to me that I could ask someone for information about Jerry's condition, or ask why he was still on a stretcher in a hallway instead of a normal room. This was Hazard. Like most people of my station in life, I felt I had no say in how systems work, no thought that you could question a situation or system. This was a hospital where those who work there know what to do.

The one change with Jerry that morning was that bubbles had formed on his lips, a visual image that has lived in my mind for sixty-five years. And my gesture: I took a tissue from a box there somewhere and as gently as I could wiped the bubbles from his lips. The only other initiative I could think to do was go out to the third floor lobby to see if I could find a phone and call our sister Gwynne to tell her about the situation. I was directed by someone to go outside to the sidewalk where there was a pay phone. I made my way down the stairs, found the phone booth and called Gwynne. For that school year, Gwynne was living with our Aunt Agnes in Winston Salem, North Carolina. I don't remember how I knew the number to call. I gave Gwynne the message that our big brother had been seriously injured in a car wreck and was in the hospital in Hazard. Around 10:30 a.m. some friends of our family, Mr. and Mrs. Bonta, came to the hospital to be with my grandmother. They asked me if I wanted to go to breakfast. We returned to the hospital less than an hour later. As I was heading up to the third floor again, I was told that Jerry had died. I remember that I was on the stairs in mid-step, my right foot on the lower step and my left foot on the upper step. Jerry's body had already been taken away.

My weeping grandmother was escorted from the hospital by Mr. and Mrs. Bonta. It was clear to me what I should do. I set out walking down Main Street and then out East Main Street the half-mile or so to the William Engle Funeral Home. My father had been sent there the year before when he died in the VA hospital. Jerry, Gwynne and I had sat together in the funeral home chapel during the services for our father.

The business at hand the day of Jerry's death was to select a casket. The decision was wholly mine. I surveyed a dozen caskets of different styles and prices. I picked a substantial one, made of black walnut. I signed a paper, shook hands with Mr. Engle, and walked to Main Street where I heard someone say as I passed by, "That's his brother."

Gwynne and I had a government-appointed lawyer named Mr. Dixon whose role was to serve as our court-appointed "Committee." He represented us as recipients of modest funds from the government because our father, a former coal miner, had been a service-connected veteran of World War II who had died the year before in the Fort Thomas, Kentucky, Veterans Hospital. Mr. Dixon was a courteous and highly respected member of the local bar. He had been a reassuring presence in our lives, dispensing $38 a month to each of the three of us. Now it would be only Gwynne and me following the death of Jerry in the auto/train collision two days before.

Gwynne, who was fourteen now, was brought to Hazard by relatives from North Carolina for Jerry's funeral, and we reunited in the Main Street hotel. On the day of the funeral, our Committee, Mr. Dixon, called to say he knew we were getting ready for Jerry's funeral but he hoped we could come to his office across the street for a few minutes before the services. It would not take long.

Mr. Dixon was an important grownup in our lives. Our financial support was administered by him so, of course, we should go. When we went to Mr. Dixon's office, there were three other men there, sitting side by side across the table, four well-dressed men counting Mr. Dixon, facing my sister and me. The men included the lawyer of the diminutive son-of-a-lawyer who had been driving the car when my brother was killed, and perhaps also the diminutive son's father himself. The three silent men in the room may all have been lawyers for all we knew, but it was hard to tell since we were not formally introduced. We did not know who the men were.

The genial Mr. Dixon began by thanking us for coming. The car in which our brother had been fatally injured had been insured for $5,000, he said. He assured us that the check we would receive would be for the full amount. He explained that in some cases families sometimes sued insurance companies for more money than the amount agreed upon in the policy but that insurance companies were very reliable in promptly paying the full amount agreed upon in the policy. It would expedite matters in the present situation if we would each sign a paper which he, Mr. Dixon, our attorney, had prepared, saying that we declined to sue the owner of the car in which our brother had been killed, or otherwise hold the diminutive driver's family responsible for Jerry's death. We followed our lawyer-guardian's recommendation, affixed our signatures to the document (receiving no copy for our own files) and left the table of well-dressed men to attend our brother's funeral. A year later we received a check for $3,800 ($5,000 minus Mr. Dixon's $1,200 fee).

Look Homeward, Angel

IN EARLY AUGUST of 1958 I drove to Avery County, North Carolina, to spend some days with my Aunt Sol before starting my senior year at the University of Kentucky. I had been working that summer as a reporter for my hometown newspaper, the *Hazard Herald*. Before leaving, I checked out *Look Homeward, Angel* from the library to read during my four mountain-cool days in the high Blue Ridge country. Aunt Sol was my mother's sister. My sister Gwynne and our older brother Jerry and I had grown up as members of our mother's large and lively ten-person family. The family members–Sol, Larry, Thelma (our mother), E.J., Mae and Maude (twins), Holly, Warren G., and Grandma and Granddad–were the primary subjects of our conversations. On this particular visit, when we were not talking about our kinfolks, I was sitting out on Sol's front porch reading about Eugene Gant and his large, loud family in Altamont. I finished reading *Look Homeward, Angel* at ten a.m. on the third day of my visit. I was so moved by the story of the Gant family, I got up from my wicker chair, told Aunt Sol I was going to drive to Asheville for the day, and set forth.

The Blue Ridge Parkway was only two miles from Sol's house, Asheville about seventy-five miles away. I'd never been on the Parkway. Driving along, looking at the far, magnificent vistas, I was literally and figuratively "in the clouds." I remember my sense of descending from a dream-like height down to the real Asheville. I say "real" but in my emotional state, the actual city was no more than a parallel universe to Thomas Wolfe's imagination. Without a street map, without asking for directions, I entered the city and drove straight to Spruce Street. I stepped out of the car and saw the Old Kentucky Home, the gabled white house, the broad porch, exactly as Wolfe had described it. I stepped onto the porch. This place, I thought. The space of it, within and outside time, the moment a mystic union of forever and of now.

I was the only visitor at that hour. The door was open but no one was present to accept my entrance fee so I went in and toured the house alone, wandering at my own pace through the rooms. The parlor, sitting rooms, the dining room, the kitchen in back, the steep stairs leading to the second floor. I felt Eugene Gant's family around me, I heard their voices, saw their faces. Every room was powerful, scenes from the novel unfolding in each one. The room where Ben died, in life and in fiction, overwhelmed me. I stood in front of the large bed where Thomas Wolfe was born and Ben had died, lost in Wolfe's descriptions, lost in the living moment, lost in the memory of my brother Jerry who had been killed in a car wreck at age eighteen.

I was sixteen when Jerry died. Tom was sixteen when Ben died. Oh lost, indeed. When I left the house I walked up Spruce Street to Pack Square and its spraying fountain. I felt the water drops on my face and arms. I felt the relief of it on a hot day. The Pack Library was across the street. I went in, told the librarian, Mrs. Champion, I was from Kentucky and that I had just read *Look Homeward, Angel*. I asked if I could see a sample of Thomas Wolfe's handwriting. She led me to a room and took out a sheaf of letters. I had finished reading *Angel* only a few hours earlier; now I sat at a library table in

Asheville, holding a letter written by Wolfe in longhand. It was a moving, almost mystical experience. The page was not an artifact but something alive and breathing as if the writer himself had placed it in my hand.

I didn't peruse the Wolfe materials very long. I couldn't take in much more. Returning the letters to Mrs. Champion's desk, we talked a few minutes. As I was about to leave, the telephone rang. Mrs. Champion answered and spoke briefly to the caller. Then I heard her say that a young man from Kentucky was there, that he admired Tom's writing and had just looked at a few of Tom's letters. The caller asked to speak to me. Handing me the telephone, Mrs. Champion whispered, "It's Mabel." Tom's sister, called Helen in the novel, said she was glad I was interested in Tom's writing, that she had been to Kentucky and would I like to come over to the Spruce Street house for afternoon tea? It was as easy to talk to her as it was to my Aunt Sol. But I was too shy to go over for tea. I said I had to get on back to Avery County. She told me to come for a visit some other time. I said I would. Mabel Wolfe Wheaton died a few weeks later.

Mr. Frost

SIX WEEKS into my college career at the University of Kentucky in 1955, I went to Robert Frost's poetry reading in Memorial Hall. I had a good seat, up front, and quite a good look at Mr. Frost. As he recited and read his poems, much of my pleasure was in recognizing poems we had so recently studied in my high school English class. I knew some of the poems by heart: "Stopping by Woods on a Snowy Evening," "The Road Not Taken," "Fire and Ice." Mr. Frost was eighty-one in 1955. I was eighteen.

Five years later, in the fall of 1960, Wallace Stegner invited our Stanford University graduate fiction writing class to his home for drinks and to meet his house guest, Robert Frost. Mr. Stegner was a prominent author of novels, stories, and essays. He was one of the most prominent environmental writers of his day. He and his wife Mary lived in an elegant house in Los Altos Hills, a rural area fairly close to Palo Alto and the Stanford campus. There were ten of us student writers at his home that evening, plus our teacher Malcolm Cowley, the noted expatriate American writer whose book *Exile's Return* chronicled "the lost generation" of American writers living in Paris after World War I. Hemingway, Dos Passos, Crane, Pound, Stein. Later a noted critic and editor at Viking Press, Mr. Cowley initiated Viking's Portable series of books. It is generally considered that his long essay introducing *The Portable Faulkner*, published in

1946, resurrected Faulkner's career and brought all of his novels back into print. Some in our student group wondered what the likes of us were doing at such an occasion. Larry McMurtry had acquired some polish along the way but Ken Kesey and I were hicks from Oregon and Kentucky. Rough colonials might be a better term. The fantasy writer Peter Beagle, from the Bronx, was the only one in our crowd who had published a novel, but at age twenty he had not been to such parties.

We guests convened about seven p.m. After sipping our drinks and munching on the hors d'oeuvres and talking among ourselves for an hour or so, Mr. Stegner asked for our attention, had us all stand and form a loose reception line. A few minutes later he returned, escorting Robert Frost into the room.

Mr. Frost was eighty-six by then and he moved slowly. Mr. Stegner guided him gently along the reception line, introducing him to the guests one by one. "And this is Mr. Norman," he said when it was my turn. Mr. Frost looked at me, sixty years his junior, nodded and said, "Mr. Norman." We shook hands. His hand was small, delicate. No introductions were necessary when he came to Malcolm Cowley. They knew each other well and when they had shaken hands they moved toward the two chairs that had been set out for them. Well, I thought, now I will hear Mr. Frost expound upon the meanings of his work. Perhaps Mr. Cowley will reveal to us young writers some details of his time in Paris with Hem and Dos that he had left out of *Exile's Return*.

But Mr. Frost and Mr. Cowley were off duty that evening. They wanted to talk to each other. Picture two distinguished senior American writers, seated in chairs drawn close together since both were hard of hearing, leaning toward each other, taking turns fairly yelling into each other's ears. This was fine with us twenty-somethings, for it made it easy to eavesdrop on their conversation.

After a second round of drinks Mr. Cowley started telling Mr. Frost about his recent experience of sitting next to Marilyn Monroe at a fancy literary banquet in New York. Mr. Frost seemed to not know who Marilyn Monroe was. "She's a glamorous movie actress," said Mr. Cowley. "Married to Arthur Miller." Mr. Frost seemed to not know who Arthur Miller was. "The writer," said Mr. Cowley. "Arthur Miller."

"Ah, yes," said Mr. Frost. "Miller." As they talked on about Miller we students glanced at each other. We knew to not interrupt the two men but we could not keep the smiles from our faces as it became clear that Mr. Frost was talking about Henry Miller and Mr. Cowley about Arthur Miller. No matter. They talked happily for a good half hour about Miller before moving on to other subjects.

Three months and some days after shaking my hand at the Stegner home, Robert Frost stepped to the podium to read a poem as part of John Kennedy's inauguration as President of the United States. Eight inches of snow had fallen in Washington the night before. It was twenty-two degrees outside and the wind was blowing. Mr. Frost looked frail and vulnerable on black and white TV but his voice was strong as he began to read from a typed sheet of paper. Suddenly a gust of wind tore the paper from his hand. Lyndon Johnson stood to assist him but the old poet waved him away. Without missing a beat Mr. Frost recited his poem. He had it in his head.

Shattered Jewel

THE SHATTERED JEWEL fractured tendencies dizzy patterns at the intersections watching the train go by quirks of light between the gons a coded message rapid word lines across the sky what could they be saying? That the world is a mysterious place and does not owe you an explanation your job is to surrender all freely give and get your story straight. Beyond the narrow doors the corridor the floor surrender all freely give across the same new sky beneath the trains the track ties manual labor put them there.

Last night you had it all figured out but now it's day and there the books still are unread body untouched unloved universal longing all over the world from childhood a wound and more than one and mental anguish questions gone unanswered death of Wilhelm Reich Jock Yablonski his family killed too much to remember that's what newspapers are for tell it one time daily knowing seven is a magic number seven days a week a better unit of measure get your story straight.

Weekly newspaper times fifty-two eight columns per page we could count the letters in their fonts something that happened one time I had written a summary of my life story ten typed pages single-spaced story touched the high spots some low spots too handset by Elzy my life-story one letter at a time ten-point Bodoni thirty column inches in a tray five-thousand letters like jewels of my life's meaning carrying it past the printing press I stepped on my own feet and down I went words and sentences Elzy's patient crafting flung like raindrops on the press room floor.

Near the end of life he wants to settle accounts and discovers they have already been settled but what about debts moral debts emotional debts? Don't worry about it, all settled you are free to go. A few items to attend to first. I wanted to plant a new dogwood tree in our family's cemetery plot. It feels strange that the tree that holds your story is rotted at the roots. I am reconciled after dropping everything that has any weight at all including seventeen pounds. I will fly away soon holding all trees in mind the fact of trees a warning to protect such trees as remain everyone knowing or should know we are in danger of living in a treeless world. And think about water. Air. Then sudden recognition that you are nowhere near ready to take a journey. What an illusion. Wishful thinking. Your trip has been postponed.

A year after the war my dad and I walking from Allais on the railroad tracks over the Allais bridge and the pedestrian bridge to the Family Theater in town comedy newsreel previews of coming attractions the movie ended my dad came out of the theater his khaki pants urine-soaked down to his knees. Dad was too old for basic training at thirty-four on five-mile runs with eighteen-year-olds but the nation seemed to need my father thirty-four-year-old coal miner wife in a mental hospital after the war he never worked again. Once he found a six-weeks job in Loraine as a janitor of an elementary school. Seventy years later I still have his pay stubs and a picture of him in his uniform in his Bible which he treasured.

Mother's high hopes declining three babies in four years from marriage to Fourth Street in ten years she suffered loudly. One morning up at 4 a.m. banging on the piano Granddad asleep before going to work at the mines yelled through the wall told Mother to hush that racket go back to bed she ignored him kept banging on the piano he leapt out of bed shoved her off the piano stool onto the floor and made her cry.

Mother on the side of the road my grandmother put her out left her behind Wilgus watches her disappear out the back car window. Mother home blue dress dark circles under her eyes a snowstorm she runs out in the middle of the night in nightgown and houseshoes claws at a stump thinking it is me frozen in the ice and snow. Next day a walk to the pasture we come back our mother is gone back to the hospital three years before I see her again.

In a car on Main Street next to the Grand Hotel watching snow fall onto the street people passing by on the sidewalks dark falling early town lights coming on I knew I'd always remember that moment Main Street a wonderland. My dad and mom carrying packages and shopping bags they seemed happy. January afternoon my dad built a sled out of an old ironing board pulled us through the snow all over Black Gold camp burned two holes in the front with a red-hot poker for the rope to go through the burned wood smell on the winter air so fresh and pure and the white snow at dusty dark like the world had been made over and everything was new again.

Granddad building the early morning fires the grates coal stove in the kitchen sound of his workboots on the snow outside as he walked past my bedroom window early morning dark to the work truck. Granddad's work clothes overalls coal dust underground mine every day inside the earth at the coal face with the crew he was the time keeper kept everybody's time then spent time with me little boy seven eight summer evenings we would go to the front yard to see the passenger plane on its way to Knoxville from Lexington where he said my mother was and my father was in their separate hospitals. Smashing whiskey bottles on the river bank striking back against the adults trying to figure out why things weren't better.

Then I remembered Uncle Delmer at the coal face drilling coalite holes in the seam when his hair got caught in the drill and pulled out a piece of his scalp and he screamed dropped the drill still running out the drift mouth yelling oh God oh God his brothers on the tipple working the shakers block and egg ten tons of block dropped into the truck Delmer behind the wheel started the engine and pulled away blood all over his face drove eight miles to town past the hospital three more miles to the mouth of Trace Fork to the yard of the house where he was born and raised twenty-eight years before his mother and sister Jenny in the yard stringing beans both screamed and cried and reached to touch him he cursed them went in the wash house tore off his work clothes got under the cold shower washed himself except his head still bleeding put on clean clothes a towel around his head climbed back in the truck headed out Trace Fork back to town where he entered the hospital and fell unconscious to the floor.

Hours later his head swathed in bandages his friend tall elegant Vera Hughes wife of lawyer Hughes explained to the doctors and nurses that she would take charge of Delmer now. Delmer accepted Vera's support and walked with her down the hall and out to her Cadillac holding hands in silence soon the two were in her brick home Delmer asleep in bed thus began a three-year experience for Delmer every bit as life changing as his three years in the Army during the war and his three-year postwar partnership with his father and brothers in the coal business. Vera was thirty-six seven years older than war veteran Delmer Collier his young nephew Wilgus was dazzled by his new aunt Vera the first grownup in his life to grant that at fourteen he was no longer a little boy the first

208

person outside the family with whom he talked about his parents his mother Alice committed to a mental hospital when Wilgus was five.

Alice to Glen, *He's a nervous little boy just now getting some rhythm in his legs. He needs to get more meat on his bones. He's got a sweet personality I adore being with him. Yesterday we spent an hour learning to skip. It was a great mystery to him at first. We worked and worked at it. He got a little frustrated sometimes but he really wanted to learn. Most of the other little kids his age around here could do it. He was so determined and brave. Then all of a sudden he was a champion skipper! Now he skips everywhere he goes and I skip along with him sometimes.*

I have been trying to get this stuff said for forty years. I have written themes articles stories essays howled at the moon a time or two letters to the editor diaries reports declarations summations and lamentations pamphlets journals letters to everybody I know and many that I do not. I have talked in tongues prayed confided confessed professed hollered yelled and whispered I have testified editorialized itemized apologized orated narrated marinated muttered and spluttered for forty years and still have managed only a minor squeak of uncertain truth.

Since we are in a confessional mood here let's face the fact that in the grand scheme of things subjectivity is as interesting and useful and important as objectivity what's going on out there is equal to what's going on in here and vice versa like helping Grandma do the family wash every Monday as a child then thinking about it for seventy years. Which approaches knowing there is a limit to your days inspires appreciation allegiance faithfulness to those and what you love all the people gone and around me still, sweet family dear friends colleagues associates the days are sweeter as there are fewer of them. Society does not exist just for the people who are alive.

209

Sunday morning Delmer leads the drunks to Trace Fork where family and friends are clearing the graveyard Blanche and Wilgus linger behind. Finally at end of day Wilgus is alone in his old home rush of memory flashes all departed family members pass in review the old house alive with voices scenes all covered over by kudzu. Now I'm going through this house. Now I'm feeling the walls of this old house. Then in the dark he walks down off the mountain down Trace Fork one more time.

Granddad looking for the old homeplace debris of the ruined mountain no visible road tall weeds choking trees pushing through the small clearing suddenly a meadow overgrown and wild the field of my mother's childhood foundation stones chimney stones wood rail fence he searches the weeds beneath a ragged tree he planted fifty years ago stands up two apples in his hand. Without speaking we eat the sweet apples, sweet apples even in the wreckage, don't give up there may be apples there.